Heidegger in Chicago

A Comedy of Errors

Jef Costello

Counter-Currents Publishing
San Francisco
2015

Copyright © 2015 by Jef Costello
All rights reserved

Cover design by
Kevin I. Slaughter

Published in the United States by
COUNTER-CURRENTS PUBLISHING LTD.
P.O. Box 22638
San Francisco, CA 94122
USA
http://www.counter-currents.com/

Hardcover ISBN: 978-1-940933-10-8
Paperback ISBN: 978-1-940933-11-5
E-Book ISBN: 978-1-940933-12-2

Library of Congress Cataloging-in-Publication Data

Costello, Jef, 1973-
  Heidegger in Chicago : a comedy of errors / Jef Costello.
    pages cm
  ISBN 978-1-940933-10-8 (hardcover : alk. paper) -- ISBN 978-1-940933-11-5 (pbk. : alk. paper)
  1. Heidegger, Martin, 1889-1976--Fiction. I. Title.

PS3603.O8675H46 2015
813'.6--dc23

2015012765

CONTENTS

Chapter 1: "L.A." 1

Chapter 2: "Neverland Ranch" 19

Chapter 3: "Vegas" 43

Chapter 4: "San Francisco" 68

Chapter 5: "New York" 89

Chapter 6: "Chicago" 115

About the Author 140

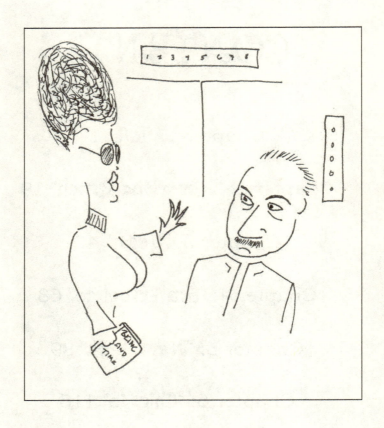

"What a doll!" thought Chinchilla Heatherton

CHAPTER ONE

"L.A."

Chinchilla Heatherton stared up at the man behind the lectern. "He reminds me of my father," she thought. He too had legs that could bend in the middle, enabling him to sit on objects smaller than himself. He too had colored orbs embedded in his head, enabling him to register light waves refracted off the surface of objects. He too had a hole below the orbs, from which sounds emerged.

But the sounds she was hearing now were not like those her father made. Those had usually been wet sounds, but these were cool and dry. As cool and dry as a fall afternoon in the Schwarzwald. She plugged another cigarette into her holder. Woodrow Hasenpfeffer leaned forward to light it. "Thank you, darling," she said languidly. The speaker glanced at her momentarily. She had been too loud, and she knew it. She was used to being the center of attention.

"My pleasure, pet," hissed Hasenpfeffer, oblivious to the audience.

Chinchilla crossed and uncrossed her legs, then pulled at the neckline of her dress, trying anything to attract the speaker's attention. She was fascinated by his exotic, peasant dress, especially by his gaiters.

"What is that he's wearing?" she whispered to Hasenpfeffer.

"I believe they call it 'the existential suit.' I imagine it will be all the rage by the time he's left L.A." Hasenpfeffer was waspish and suave. Tall, with a thin moustache, impeccable taste in clothes, and brilliantined, black hair, he too had legs that could bend in the middle.

The speaker finished his presentation. Chinchilla, mesmerized, forgot to applaud until seconds after she realized that others were clapping and that some had even risen to their feet. The question period began as soon as the clamor had died down.

"Professor Heidegger, could you explain the ontological difference again, please?" someone asked. Patiently, Heidegger explained once more, speaking in the same monotone Chinchilla had found so hypnotic, and powerfully attractive. She imagined that he was addressing his answers to her and only to her, though she had said nothing.

She searched and searched for something to ask him. Finally, she had an inspiration and shot her hand up. He called on her. "Professor Heidegger," she said, "do you believe in gay marriage?"

Heidegger thought for a moment, then began speaking. Chinchilla listened intently, more earnestly than she had ever listened to anything before in her life. Her moist, glossy lips parted a bit. She forgot to breathe. This man had her so thoroughly in his spell. He went on, and just when she thought he was finished, he added something. The answer had gone beyond her question entirely, to get at the very basis from which such a question could be asked—to something Heidegger kept calling "originary." The sounds washed over her, and she felt something vibrating at her core, as if the words he used touched her not through their meaning but through sound alone. He finished and went on to another questioner. Chinchilla had not understood a word he had said.

She began to feel faint. For a split second it crossed her mind that if she did faint, Heidegger would definitely have to respond. He would rush to her side. She would reach up, clutching at the little oak leaf and acorn patterns embroidered into his lapels. Suddenly, she was Camille. She was Garbo. She was dying. Heidegger was Robert Taylor. A last kiss? Chinchilla shook herself out of this reverie. But she had to get out—she had to get air. She rose abruptly, heading down the aisle and to the doors which led into the hotel lobby. Hasenpfeffer quickly followed her. "What is it, my dear?" he implored her.

"God I'm beginning to hate him!" she thought to herself. She had allowed Woodrow Hasenpfeffer to court her for the last two years, mainly because he had his own jet. She had the house in Bel Aire, the condo in Malibu. There were occasional TV appearances, and the residuals from that go-dawful show her agent had made her do in the '60s, the one where she was shipwrecked on an island with six other has-been actors. Her five-day marriage to Count Massimo Chimichanga had ended in divorce and a hefty settlement, but she had run through that in one afternoon spent on Rodeo Drive.

Outside the meeting room, Chincilla sat down in a red velvet chair and reached for another cigarette.

"Do you need some water?" Hasenpfeffer inquired.

"I need a drink," she snapped, and soon they were sitting in front of matching drinks in the hotel bar: Bloody Marys with huge stalks of celery. "Tabasco!" shrieked Chinchilla in the direction of the waiter. "I just don't get it," she whispered. "I don't know what it is about this guy. I've tried Satanism, Objectivism, EST, Scientology, the Kabbalah, and lesbianism—in that order—but somehow this is different. Just the title of that book, *Being and Time* . . . it hit me when I saw that title. I just knew: this is the guy."

Two weeks earlier, she had entered a bookstore in Beverly Hills, wearing a long, camel's hair coat with its high collar turned up, and large amber-colored sunglasses—even though it had been years since anyone had recognized her. Oh, and the black leather driving gloves. She never took them off. Liver spots.

Chinchilla moved through the store slowly and cautiously, as if she were poised to flee at any moment. When a large man in a dress shirt with wet armpits glanced in her direction she lifted a hand up to hide her face and then turned down the philosophy aisle. She knew where the philosophy books were only because they were on the other side of the General Metaphysics section, which she occasionally visited. And that was when she saw *Being and Time*: the attractive, hardcover Macquarrie and Robinson translation. Something about the cover of the book spoke to her. She bought it and left hurriedly, as if expecting paparazzi to descend on her at any moment.

Chinchilla began reading the book by the pool that afternoon, while sipping a Long Island Iced Tea. She started with the table of contents, and began pondering the book's strange vocabulary. She knew something about Being from her experience with EST. "Being alive . . . being alive," she whispered to herself and sipped her drink. The straw made a rude gurgling, sucking sound, and she realized the glass was empty. She set it down on the metal patio table with a loud BANG. "Time," she intoned, and lay the book against her breasts. "Being and time. . . . Like the sands of the hourglass, these are the days of our lives."

Heidegger in Chicago

But what on earth did "Dasein" mean?

Her thoughts now turned from the book to its author. She imagined Heidegger with a dark, angular face, a beret perched slightly askew on the top of his head. She pictured him smoking those very strong French cigarettes her husband, the Count, had enjoyed. Heidegger was sitting outdoors at a café, scribbling in a notebook. There was a demitasse at one of his elbows, a plate with some kind of . . . French . . . cheese or something at his other elbow. It was 1940. Heidegger was a philosopher by day, a member of the Underground, fighting the Nazis by night. She could hear the sound of jackboots approaching the café. Heidegger quickly closed his book, took a carrier pigeon from his coat pocket, a tiny scroll already tied to one of its talons, and released it into the bright sky. An SS officer with a dueling scar took aim, fired, and missed.

Chinchilla was angry at herself for daydreaming again. She glanced down at the table of contents, and was pleased to see that Heidegger included a discussion of Care. Care was very important to Chinchilla. She opposed Hate in all its ugly forms. "He must be a wonderful man," she thought. "What does it take to write something like this?" She hefted the book in her left hand. Five-hundred and eighty-nine pages. Chinchilla couldn't imagine reading a book that long, let alone writing one. Then it occurred to her that this might be yet another of

"L.A."

those books that she had bought and never finished. "Not this time," she said, out loud. She thought that the book might become for her something like the Bible was for others. She would leave it by her bed. She would read a few passages each night before retiring, and go to bed feeling inspired by its wisdom.

Something startled her, and she realized that her houseboy, Hop Theng, was at her side, removing the drink from the table. "You want another, Countess?" he asked, sounding like he had a mouth full of shot. "No," she said, distinctly annoyed. He walked around the pool to the French doors and suddenly drew back, calling to her, "Oh! Mr. Hasenpfeffer here to see you!" Woodrow Hasenpfeffer emerged from the house into the bright sun, waving to her. He was wearing a pin-striped, double-breasted suit and a bright grin. "Hello, lovely one!" he called, striding around the pool. Chinchilla didn't want to see him, not now. Not when . . . Well, it seemed silly to think that a book could make her not want to see Hasenpfeffer. But it was more than the book. It was as if Heidegger himself had come between them. She wanted to hide *Being and Time* before Hasenpfeffer could set his jaded, unsavory eyes on it.

"What's that you're reading? *Being and Time*? Oh, my! Philosophy, Chinchilla? You're not serious!" he smiled and diddled with his moustache.

She turned her head away. "What do you want, Bunny?" she asked, needling him with his Harvard nickname.

But he wouldn't let the subject drop. "You're really reading that book? You know, my nephew teaches philosophy at UCLA. He told me this Heidegger fellow is coming here next week. The name meant nothing to me, but apparently he's the next big thing."

Chinchilla sat forward quickly. "What did you say? He's coming here?"

"Yes, to give some sort of lecture. He's on a whirlwind tour of several major American cities."

For the next seven days, Chinchilla Heatherton could think of nothing other than meeting Heidegger. The day after Hasenpfeffer had given her the news, she stood in front of the full length mirror in her bedroom, wearing her nightgown, and her heart sank. "I'm not ready," she said to herself. "I'm not ready. . . . But damn it I will be!" She rushed over to her bedside, picked up the white, enamel receiver of her princess phone, and dialed. "Hello, Margo? What was the name of that woman who gave you the chelated seaweed-guava eyelid treatment?" She twirled the cord around in her fingers and, looking down, realized that she would have to go on wearing the driving gloves. "Does she do Black Sea salt scrubbing? Or Dead Sea, or whatever it is? . . . Yes . . . Good."

The arrival of the chelated seaweed-guava

"L.A."

eyelid woman began a daily round of therapists, masseurs, natural healers, and plastic surgeons. Chinchilla was massaged, waxed, and scrubbed. She underwent colonic irrigation, neti nasal douching, ear candling, crystal therapy, aroma therapy, essential oil therapy, Reiki, Rolfing, past life regression, fasting, foot reflexology, Tai Chi, Chee Gung, Hatha Yoga, dermabrasion, botox, and Scientological clearing. She was quietly escorted out of a Lamaze class.

At the end of five days, Chinchilla was so exhausted she began leafing through the "spa getaway" brochures Margo had leant her, until she realized that that meant doing it all over again.

On day six, she rested. Hasenpfeffer called her at noon. "The Countess is asleep," Hop Theng told him.

He called back at 2:00. "Hello . . . yes," Chinchilla whispered, lifting her heated eye mask.

"Tomorrow is the big day, my sweet," Hasenpfeffer said. "I still don't understand why you want to meet this man." He waited for a response, but none came. "I'd be delighted to escort you to the lecture, though."

"When is it?"

"Tomorrow at 7:00 p.m. at the airport Marriott."

She was glad it wasn't in the morning. "Do you know what the lecture is about?"

"Well, I have a flyer. They were handing them out at the M-G-M commissary this morning. It's a damnably strange title. 'What is Dwelling?'"

"What did you ask me?" Chinchilla said, sitting up and wondering where Hop Theng was with her coffee.

"No, that's the title, dear. 'What is Dwelling?' I don't know what it means either."

"Dwelling," Chinchilla thought. "Dwelling on your problems, I would think. It's about learning to take one day at a time, and to be . . . proactive. Yes, it's a self-help talk." She hoped it would be easier to understand than *Being and Time*. Two days earlier she had returned to the bookstore and bought another volume by Heidegger: *Basic Problems of Phenomenology*. Hasenpfeffer's nephew, the philosophy professor, had advised her that this was easier than *Being and Time*. But Chinchilla couldn't understand it either. She imagined the lecture would reveal all.

And now it was over, and Chinchilla still did not understand. She sipped her Bloody Mary, wishing that Hasenpfeffer would just disappear. Suddenly, there was a great deal of hubbub from outside the bar. The lecture audience was leaving. Chinchilla brightened. After they had all left, she might go back to the room and talk alone with Heidegger. But then she realized that the little German was in the midst of the crowd that now moved through the lobby, being peppered with questions. He was moving toward the elevators. Chinchilla caught a glimpse of his face. He looked exhausted and annoyed. She real-

"L.A."

ized he was probably heading for his room. If Heidegger disappeared upstairs, she might never get a chance to speak with him alone.

She pushed through the crowd. "Excuse me! Excuse me! I'm the Contessa Chinchilla Heatherton!" But no one appeared to notice her. Heidegger was entering an elevator alone, waving the crowd away with a polite, but weary smile. Chinchilla pushed past a large man wearing Vulcan ears and got on the elevator just as the doors were about to close.

Now she was alone with Heidegger. He stood stiffly, looking down at the floor. Just once, he glanced up in her direction with a slight twinkle in his eyes.

"What a doll!" thought Chinchilla. And she couldn't take her eyes off his existential suit. In this new light, she could see that it was dark green, and not the grey she had thought it was earlier. Heidegger had not pressed one of the elevator buttons. "Oh, what's your floor?" she asked brightly and, when he answered her, she pressed 21. "That's my floor too! What a coincidence!" she said and began giggling, then playfully slapped Heidegger on the arm. He twinkled at her again, then cleared his throat, bringing his fist up to his lips.

There was silence for several seconds.

"Are you in town long?" Chinchilla asked him. He answered politely, but concisely that he was leaving the following day. Chinchilla froze. She could think of nothing else to say. She was amazed that Heidegger had not shown more interest in her. Most men would have.

The doors opened and Heidegger, with a slight bow, insisted that she leave first.

"Well, good night!" said Chinchilla. She walked deliberately in the opposite direction. As soon as Heidegger's back was turned, however, she did an about face and squinted to see what door he was headed toward. He inserted a plastic key in his lock, and just as he opened the door, Chinchilla sprinted several feet ahead and saw that the number was 2123. Heidegger had been unaware of her approach, and shut the door gently.

Just as Chinchilla was about to walk back down the hall and formulate Plan B, the door to the room next to Heidegger's opened and out stepped Tyler Hasenpfeffer, the gay philosophy professor nephew of Woodrow Hasenpfeffer.

"Tyler!" Chinchilla cried, "What are you doing here?"

"Shoosh! Not so loud," he said and quickly turned to shut the door behind him. But Chinchilla had seen into the room and what it contained.

"Tyler, what are you doing in there!"

He hushed her again. "Keep your voice down. I don't want the old man to hear us."

"What is going on here?" she demanded.

"Well, all right. I'll show you. But you have to keep it a complete secret." Chinchilla promised that she would, and Tyler un-

"L.A."

locked the door and motioned for her to come in. There was a desk against the wall separating Tyler's room from Heidegger's. The desk was piled high with sophisticated electronic equipment. Something that appeared to be a thin metal tube had been driven into the wall separating Tyler's room from Heidegger's.

"What is all this?" Chinchilla asked, and then she saw the TV monitor. It showed a man in front of a queen size bed, taking off his jacket. It was Heidegger!

"I've bored a hole in Heidegger's wall, and inserted a tiny camera through it so that we can see into his room. I can see—and videotape—everything that happens," Tyler said with a self-satisfied smirk.

"But . . . why?"

"So that I can out him."

Chinchilla suddenly remembered what Bunny had told her about Tyler. He had made a small name for himself in something called "Queer Theory," and had published a book a couple of years earlier called *Buridan's Asshole*. It had purported to "out" many a famous philosopher as gay. Recently, Tyler had turned to outing living philosophers. "Yessirree," he said. "I can see everything that goes on in there. This was the baby I used to out A. J. Ayer," he said, patting the VCR. "You'll never believe what Ayer is into."

Chinchilla reared back. "You mean you think that Heidegger is . . . gay?" Revealingly, she laid her right hand over her heart.

"Well . . . no," Tyler said, looking down. "That is, I really don't know. He could be. People have their suspicions. You should hear some of the things Michel Foucault has to say about him."

"No, it's impossible!" Chinchilla cried. "He's a sexy, vibrant, virile man. He's got a sort of, I don't know, Burl Ives quality. Only he's so European or something. Anyway, it's scary how sexy he is."

Tyler curled his lip. "You just can't believe that a masculine man could be gay."

"I'll prove to you he's not gay," she said, thumping the carpet with one of her heels.

"What are you going to do?"

But Chinchilla didn't answer. She left hurriedly, and, moments later, Tyler heard her knocking at Heidegger's door.

Several minutes earlier, Heidegger had unpacked a compact, beige suitcase and had removed two small, stuffed animals: a rabbit and a mole. He went everywhere with them. They were called Rabbit Podvillion and Mole Bracegirdle. Heidegger had gotten the idea from Fritz Lang, who went everywhere with a stuffed monkey. Sometimes, Heidegger would talk to them after a long day of writing or speaking. Once Hans-Georg Gadamer had shown up unannounced at the Todtnauberg hut, obviously tripping on acid, and had carried on a long conversation with the two animals. Chinchilla and Tyler had not noticed Heidegger setting the rabbit and the mole on the dresser in his room. They had been too busy arguing.

Now Heidegger answered his door, coming face to face once again with Chinchilla Heatherton. She had yanked the neckline of her dress down a bit just as the door swung open. "Hello . . . Professor Heidegger? I just wanted to come by and tell you . . . tell you how much I enjoyed your lecture. It was so, so . . . philosophical. And really," she grinned broadly and scratched at her cheek with long, red-shellacked nails, "really it was so . . . relevant." Something made her stop. Perhaps it was his glassy stare. Perhaps it was what she interpreted as a "smoldering look" behind the glassiness. Years later, she would write the following in her autobiography, *Tinseltown Goddess* (Feral House, 2004):

> There was a cigarette dangling from his lips. "Aren't you Chinchilla Heatherton, 'Cinammon' from *Hoolihan's Atoll*? You know, 'the movie star?'"
>
> "Why yes, I am," I said, and stepped into the room. In seconds, I was coming out of my dress. He was breathing against my shoulder, hot and heavy. "Yes!" I screamed, overcome with lust. "Give me your Dasein!"
>
> "I will give you Dasein!" he cried, snapping his suspenders.
>
> Then we were in the bed, coupling like two bison in heat. "More German!"

I screamed. He bit into the nape of my neck and began muttering a stream of German obscenity. *"Sorge! Gerade! Sein! Welt! Gestell! Gelassenheit!"* Suddenly, he went rigid, and then he screamed, *"Geworfenheit!!"*

Alas, none of this actually occurred. It was simply the product of a ghost writer's imagination.

"May I come in?" Chinchilla asked, forcing her way past him. Heidegger shut the door behind her. Chinchilla glanced briefly at the mole and the rabbit on the dresser. She took a cigarette from a pack in her bag. Heidegger lit it gallantly. "Nice place you've got here," she said, and coughed on the smoke. "So when are you going back to Amsterdam?"

They made small talk for several minutes. Heidegger glanced occasionally at the clock over her shoulder. She interpreted this as sexual tension. "Listen," Chinchilla said, "I've got something to show you." She took a videocassette from her purse. On it was a label that read *Hoolihan's Atoll.* Fortunately, the TV in Heidegger's room had a VCR built into it. Chinchilla inserted the tape into the machine, causing the TV screen to blink on. Heidegger, who had never watched television before, sat down on the edge of the bed, mesmerized. Chinchilla appeared on screen, looking twenty years younger and wearing a skintight, red sequined gown. The tape was a compilation of her best moments from the

"L.A."

series. The first scene had her as one of three participants in an island beauty contest.

Chinchilla began to babble as the images flickered on the screen. "I didn't want to do this show. I felt it . . . compromised my craft. I needed something that would stretch me as an actress. I tried to get better scripts. There was this episode where we did a musical version of *Macbeth* . . . Oh, yeah! That's what you're seeing right now. See, that's me doing the "out, out damned spot" routine to the tune of "Away in a Manger." At least I got to sing. I'm not bad, don't you think?"

Suddenly there was a crash. Chinchilla and Heidegger turned in time to see the door flying in, knocked off its hinges. They caught a glimpse of two dark figures wearing gas masks, and then the room was full of grey smoke. The two intruders lobbed gas grenades onto the carpet. Heidegger remained sitting on the bed, but his mouth opened slightly in surprise. Chinchilla screamed and backed toward the window. The intruders were carrying semi-automatic pistols fitted out with shoulder stocks and silencers.

The room began spinning, and all at once Chinchilla felt better than she had felt since . . . since . . . Her face met the plush, beautiful, comfortable carpet, that felt *so* good, and just as she lost consciousness she thought she had to find out where to get this stuff . . .

Heidegger hit the carpet seconds after she did.

Heidegger in Chicago

"This is Karl-Heinz Rudiger Gunther Schraeling. The Famous nineteenth-century German Philosopher."

CHAPTER TWO
"Neverland Ranch"

When Heidegger awakened, he thought that someone was slapping him on his left cheek. Then he realized that he was lying on a vinyl car seat, and the car was going down a bumpy road.

It was night. Heidegger sat up slowly. His limbs were stiff. He had no idea how long he had been out, and couldn't remember the events leading up to his losing consciousness. He was in the back seat of the car. In the front was a middle-aged black couple. The man was driving. The woman looked in Heidegger's direction. She was wearing bright red lip gloss. When she saw Heidegger, her eyes went wide, and she turned to the driver.

"He's waking up!"

"Shut up!" the man said. Then, without taking his eyes from the road, he called back to Heidegger. "All right, you. Listen up. You're our son, Cliotus. You're eleven years old, got it?"

Heidegger couldn't speak. He mumbled something and rubbed his head. It was then that he realized he had been stripped of his existential suit. He was wearing a white tee shirt (emblazoned with the words "STRUT FOR A CURE"), bright red shorts, and sneakers.

"I said, got it?" the man repeated. Heidegger was still unable to answer. "We're taking you to see a very famous entertainer. You'll have a very good time. Just don't say anything. You've got throat cancer, okay?" After a pause, he raised his voice and bellowed, "Do you understand me?!"

"Honey, he's German," the woman said. "I don't think he understands any English."

The situation made no sense to Heidegger, and his imperfect English did indeed make it difficult for him to understand what was happening to him. However, he realized one thing with perfect clarity: he was being kidnapped. But could an elderly German philosopher really be passed off as an eleven-year-old, black cancer patient? That was evidently what this mad pair intended to do.

Heidegger sat up and scanned the road for other cars. He could roll the window down and try and signal to one and get help. But there were no other vehicles on the road. They were driving in the country, and the car was slowing down. Heidegger saw that they had arrived at a huge, wrought-iron gate. There was a large sign on the gate which bore a skull and cross bones and the words "NO TRESPASSING!" Cameras were mounted on either side. As the car came to a stop, security guards appeared.

Heidegger's male kidnapper rolled down the window. "Mr. and Mrs. Berry and son Cliotus," he said. One of the guards bent down, looked right at Heidegger, and leered. The gates opened with a low, electronic hum, and they were waved on.

Presently, Heidegger could see that they were approaching a huge, Victorian mansion lit by floodlights. There was a large flower bed set before the main entrance, with the flowers arranged to spell out "NEVERLAND RANCH." A tall man dressed entirely in black emerged from the house and opened the car doors for them. His face was grim, until he peered into the back seat and saw Heidegger. "Well, hi Cliotus!" he said, in a syrupy tone. But when the door was pulled open and the light in the top of the car went on, illuminating Heidegger's features, the man's smile vanished. Soon another servant had appeared, and he saw to the removal of the luggage from the trunk. Berry looked down at Heidegger as they approached the front steps. "No funny business," he whispered, but Heidegger did not hear him.

Another servant—this time a tall, gaunt woman in a khaki warm-up suit—greeted them at the door. She grasped Berry's hand with a strength that made him wince. "Mr. and Mrs. Berry, I am Bertha Kittridge, Mr. Jackson's nurse. Won't you please come this way." She put her arms around the Berrys and directed them into the east wing of the house, which was furnished to look like a hunting lodge except that everything was done in hot pink. Even the moose heads were pink. Evelyn Berry turned around and saw that Heidegger was being led in the opposite direction by the manservant who had greeted them at the car.

"It's all right, Mrs. Berry," said Bertha Kittridge. "Cliotus is being escorted to the Imagination Wing. He'll be well taken care of. Now let me show you to your quarters. You must have had a long journey. I've prepared some injections that will help you sleep soundly."

Heidegger's eyes grew wide at the scene which now confronted him. The walls were lined with candy-stripes. A forest of enormous false lollipops sprouted up from the rainbow-streaked carpet. They passed through a doorway flanked by two teddy bears the size of garbage trucks, and then entered another hall. Heidegger heard something that sounded like running water. At the far end of the passage, something dark and brown was shimmering, and a familiar odor tickled Heidegger's nose. The passage wound through another forest of huge, multicolored lollipops.

Suddenly, a tall figure, probably male, stepped into the passageway from one of the side doors. It was wearing a black shirt, untucked and billowing out over the slacks. A wide-brimmed fedora adorned the head, but the face was covered by a surgical mask.

"Neverland Ranch"

Heidegger could see that the figure's features were very white. Both hands, one of which sported a glove, were now outstretched to welcome him. "Colitis!" the man cried.

"Cliotus," the servant corrected, clearing his throat.

"Cliotus," the masked man purred. He indicated the shimmering wall of brown behind him. "I suppose you're wondering about this. It's a chocolate cataract! It leads to my very own chocolate river. Why don't you take a sip? Go ahead, it's there to be enjoyed." Heidegger declined by shaking his head. The figure moved closer to him. The gloved hand came out and began massaging his left shoulder. "Alright," the man said, in his unusually high-pitched, childlike voice. "Perhaps these are more to your liking." He indicated the lollipops. "I know what you're thinking," he said. "Are they real?" Suddenly, he stretched his arms to the sky and, in a tone of exaltation cried, "Yes! Yes, they are! Go and lick one."

Again, Heidegger shook his head.

"Lick one!" the man cried, his voice still jubilant. He moved to the one nearest him and motioned for Heidegger to follow, but when the philosopher did not respond he grew impatient. "Lick it! Come over here and lick it!" he commanded. "All right, I'll show you how it's done," he said, and licked the lollipop himself. "Mmm, watermelon!"

Then he moved back over to Heidegger

and slowly removed the surgical mask. "I . . . am Michael." His face was peculiar. It was preternaturally pale, but the features did not look like they belonged to any particular race. It looked like the face of an extraterrestrial, masquerading as how he thought a typical human might appear. In particular, the nose was oddly formed. Perhaps the man noticed the way Heidegger was staring at the nose, or perhaps he was puzzled by the fact that Heidegger did not immediately respond to his name. (*Michael? Wer ist Michael?* thought Heidegger.) In any case, the man put his hands on his hips, and in an exasperated tone stated, "I'm Michael Jackson."

Still Heidegger did not respond.

The servant, who had been behind Heidegger all the while, said, "Perhaps it's the drugs."

Jackson's face took on a horrified expression. "You mean you've already . . . ."

"No. The chemo. The cancer treatment."

"Oh!" Jackson seemed relieved. He bent down to put his face close to Heidegger's and said, "I'll bet you're feeling nauseous. Well, anytime you feel like eating something just tell me. We can make anything here— *anything.*"

Heidegger *was* feeling a bit peckish. It had probably been hours since he had eaten anything. It could have been days, since he had no idea how much time had elapsed since he had been kidnapped. He turned to the servant and ordered rouladen, a side of red cabbage, a pint of Warsteiner, and, for dessert, strudel. The servant stared down at him uncomprehendingly, then turned the same expression toward Jackson, who said, "Well, you heard him. Make it!" And the servant disappeared down the passageway.

Jackson now put his arm around Heidegger's shoulders and began leading him toward the chocolate cataract, at which they took a right, and entered another passageway. "I want to show you my world, Clitoris. It's not like the world out there. It's a safe place, a place you can trust. You feel safe with me, don't you?" He didn't wait for Heidegger to respond. "It's good to have someone in your life you can trust. You can't trust your parents. I trusted mine. And look what happened? They were the organ grinder, and I was the monkey. That was my whole childhood. The worst mistake you can make is to listen to your parents, especially when they warn you not to trust other people. They're just jealous. They don't want you to have other people who love you."

Suddenly Heidegger heard a tremendous roar. It was, unmistakably, the roar of an Indian elephant. Presently they came to a pair of enormous, glass doors, at least ten feet high, and rounded at the top. Two servants in clown costumes stood beside each door.

Jackson looked down at Heidegger. Again, he stretched his arms up to heaven. "I want to show you the most wondrous place on earth!"

The clowns now reached out to open the two doors, simultaneously squeezing the bulbs on the bicycle horns strapped to their waists. With two simultaneous HONKS! The doors opened and Heidegger was hit with an assault of noise. It sounded as if they had suddenly been transported into the jungle. Heidegger heard elephants, tropical birds, monkeys, and hyenas. "We've just been through the Imaginarie, now tour the Menagerie!" Jackson cried. His arm had moved lower down Heidegger's back.

The room they now entered was a vast gallery. A concourse cut through the center of it, at least thirty feet wide. On either side were large, glass-fronted pens for the animals. The first one they came to, on the left, contained the monkeys. There were five chimpanzees. The pen was carefully designed to give the animals a sense of being back in their own habitat. There were rocks, bushes, and a large, artificial tree in the center. One chimp was seated on a high branch, and two were swinging from branches below that one. Jackson came up to the glass so close that his nose pressed against it. "Hello, Bubbles. Hello . . ." Jackson stopped short. He reached up to the center of his face, as if adjusting something, then continued. "Hello Ping-Pong. Hello Diddles . . ."

Heidegger was staring across the room at

the stark-white igloo pen that contained seventeen king penguins. "Cleetus, look!" Jackson scolded. Jackson was making kissing noises at the chimps. Suddenly, two of them jumped off the tree and began scooping up handfuls of feces and hurling it at the glass. "Eueww!!" cried Jackson. He quickly guided Heidegger toward the hyena pen. One of the clowns approached and whispered to Jackson: "Miss Kittridge is asking to speak with you." Jackson kneeled down and clasped Heidegger's cheeks in his hands. "Cleanthes, I have to make a phone call. I'll be right back." And he disappeared down a side passageway.

Jackson approached a clean, featureless stretch of oak paneling. "Open says me!" he cried. A section of the paneling suddenly sank into the wall and slid upwards, revealing a small closed-circuit monitor, a speaker, and a microphone. The screen flickered to life and, abruptly, Bertha Kittridge's flat, unadorned face appeared.

"Progress report!" commanded Jackson.

"The subjects are sleeping peacefully, sir," Kittridge answered.

"Have you successfully extracted the marrow?"

"Yes, sir. The woman was a match, Mr. Jackson. We have obtained a sufficient quantity."

"Excellent!" Jackson exclaimed, smiling. "I want that smoothie on my bedside table by 9:00 p.m." He whistled "Camptown Races," and the panel closed over the TV screen. Jackson turned to rejoin Heidegger, who he found had advanced to the final, and largest of the pens, containing two elephants.

Jackson came up behind him and placed his hand just above Heidegger's left buttock. "There's one more thing you need to see." He walked past the elephant pen, for it was not quite the last exhibit in the gallery. At the very back of the gallery, past the bestiary, was a large, glass case.

"Come," said Jackson, curling a finger at Heidegger. In the glass case was the mummy of man, dressed in a black suit of a style common in the nineteenth century. He was seated on a red velvet upholstered chair, his shriveled gray hands laid casually on his knees.

"Do you recognize him?" Jackson asked.

Heidegger did find something rather familiar about the mummy.

"This is Karl-Heinz Rudiger Gunther Schraeling, the famous nineteenth-century German philosopher."

Yes, that was it! Heidegger could dimly make out Schraeling's features in the mummy's shriveled grapefruit of a face. Schraeling had been the first philosopher ever photographed. His son Guntram had persuaded him to sit for one of the early daguerreotypes.

Schraeling had been educated at Jena, where he had heard Hegel's lectures on the history of philosophy. He had then submitted a dissertation entitled "On the Myriad Senses of Senses of Myriad." A member of the school of "Young Schleiermacherites," Schraeling had spent a year in Tübingen as a private tutor to the four children of the exiled Count Zippo of Bohemia. There, he had begun an intense study of Otto Pap, the medieval German mystic who had proclaimed that "God is a shave and a hot towel." But it would be two years before he would begin his masterwork, *Outline of My System of the Science of Ontology of the Subjective Inner Ground of the Distinction of all Objects into Spirit, Representation, Freedom, and Pure Manifestation* (or the *Outline*, for short). In the meantime, he had married Ursula von Sauerkatze, the daughter of his landlady, and had become headmaster of a reformatory in lower Saxony.

The *Outline* was printed in 1830. Because Schraeling had published the work anonymously, there was much speculation as to its authorship. Many attributed it to Hegel, because of its style. However, when Hegel declared that he could not understand it, the anonymous author was hailed as a genius. A month after the first, wildly positive reviews were published, Schraeling revealed himself as the author, to great acclaim. A glorious career had been launched.

For five years, Schraeling remained silent. Many speculated that he was afraid to publish, since anything he produced would be judged against the standard of the *Outline*.

In 1835, however, he brought out *Foundations of Right and Left Elucidated Through the Closed Chemism of Phenomenology, with a note on the System-Program of 1805, as Hallucinated by Hölderlin and Found Inside an Autopsied Consumptive.* This work was even less understood. It was not long before the call came from Berlin.

Cholera had brought an end to Hegel's reign in Berlin as Germany's leading philosopher. He had been replaced by Schelling, whose "Lectures on the Philosophy of Mythology" had been attended not only by students, but by merchants, aristocrats, clergy, soldiers, farmers, bakers, athletes, coolies, prostitutes, abortionists, thugs, and castrati. Unfortunately, Schelling, in a running feud with time, had scheduled his classes to begin promptly at 3:00 p.m., and to end promptly at 1:00 p.m. of the same day. Few were able to keep up with this rigorous schedule, and, at the end of five years, even Schelling was forced to admit that his stint in Berlin had been a failure.

Schraeling was called to be his replacement. By this time, he had fathered seventeen children by Ursula. Two had died of scarlet fever, three of neglect, another two of acute dyspepsia, and one of ennui. The remaining nine went without names for several years before Schraeling could deduce them. There was also an illegitimate child, Bubi, who later achieved notoriety as the first openly gay town crier of Erlangen. The mother of this child was unknown for many years, but scholars now believe it was none other than Princess Alexandra von Sexe-Holstein-Moocow. The evidence for this is the dedication page of Schraeling's first publication after coming to Berlin: *The Critique of Intuitions of Essence Drawn Through a Thin Reed and Folded Lengthwise, Then Cooked Until Tender In The Identity of Being and Nothing, With Ten Dialogues Between Alphonse and Gaston.* The dedication read simply "To A." Interestingly, this dedication is the only evidence we have that any such person as Princess Alexandra existed. All birth records in Sexe-Holstein-Moocow were destroyed in the event which has come to be known to historians as the "great enthusiasm" of 23 April 1812.

Schraeling had begun his stay in Berlin with an inaugural address before the entire university, as well as many of the luminaries of Berlin society. Entitled "A Clear-As-Glass Explanation of My System of Philosophy, With All Ambiguity Removed, So That Even Imbeciles and Spastics Can Understand It," the address had begun promptly at 8:00 a.m. The mood of the crowd was good, and they listened to Schraeling in absolute silence. At around noon, however, the crowd began to get restless. At 2:00 p.m., a catcall was heard from the balcony, but Schraeling seemed not to notice and continued reading. It was at this point that his pants fell down.

Schraeling often absentmindedly left home

in the morning without his belt, his shoes, his shirt, and his hat—and sometimes did not leave home at all and imagined he had walked a great distance while washing himself. Outside the hall, the ushers mistook the laughter of the crowd for threatening cries, and sealed the doors with enormous beams. At 6:00 p.m., a foul stench rose up, and rats were seen streaming out of the hall and into the courtyard through gaps in the walls. Screams were heard, but, fearing a riot, the ushers were too nervous to act. Inside the lecture hall, a horrific spectacle was unfolding. As Schraeling continued to read, many in the audience fainted. A pregnant woman went into labor. An old man had a heart attack. Graf Alois von Gliedsaugen had brought several of his children with him, and in a matter of hours these scions of the aristocracy had been reduced to beggary, and were seen calling plaintively for a few morsels of food. Others were reduced to buggery. One man went raving mad listening to Schraeling. At 4:00 p.m. the following day, Schraeling looked up from his text and asked if the audience had any questions. As there were none, he stepped down from the podium, and headed to the door, almost slipping in some fecal matter on the way. At just the moment he reached the doors, the ushers removed the bars and unsealed the room. Schraeling walked nonchalantly home.

He began a series of well-received lectures on ontology the following Monday, but the events surrounding the inaugural address cast something of a pall over his first year in Berlin. Schraeling published nothing for seven years, and instead lectured on a remarkable variety of subjects. Religion, the history of philosophy, politics, art, animal husbandry, botany, yodeling, badminton, leeching, and masturbation (or "self abuse"), were just some of his topics Schaeling took up in those fertile years. Most of these lectures have now been published. Several consist of Schraeling's own notes, combined with student comments (or "additions"; *Zusätze*) culled from class notebooks. Several others, however, contain no original words of Schraeling's at all, but are entirely made up of student comments about other student comments. A typical page from the *Lectures on Yodeling* reads as follows:

[Yodeling In the First Determination of its Concept]

[Division I:]

Addition [Zusatz] A. I don't understand what he's talking about.
Addition B: *Why* he's talking about it is the real issue . . .
Addition C: Professor Doctor Braunschweig says he's the greatest genius ever to lecture in Berlin.
Addition D:
(a) What does Braunschweig know?

(b) He's an old fool anyway.
(g) He's even harder to understand than Schraeling.
Addition E: No he's not.
Addition F: Do you want to go out for a few beers after this is over?

After completing what would be his final series of talks, the seminal *Lectures on the Phenomenology of a Woodcock*, Schraeling fell silent for thirty minutes. When he at last remerged into the public eye, he had undergone a change in his thought scholars now refer to as "the twisting." His next work shocked his followers, and delighted his detractors. It was, of course, the epochal *Zalmoxis Was Here*. In it, Schraeling had abandoned philosophical prose altogether and had written instead in the style of a parable. The first paragraph is justly celebrated:

> When the moon did gleam its blue-grey glow over the hearths and tops of the townsmen's caps, Zalmoxis came down from the mountain. Over the loch and through the heather he went, playing the clan lament. And when he came upon the town, he lit a lantern and went amongst the people crying "I seek dog! I seek dog! Where is my dog?" As there were many Chinamen about at the time he was mightily afeared. The people pointed at him and laughed.

"Where did your dog go? Did he get lost?" "Yes," said Zalmoxis. Then he began posting signs offering a reward in exchange for the return of the dog, who was called Putzi. As the first rays of the sun began to climb over the horizon, Zalmoxis started back for the mountain. "Can it be," he thought, "that these people haven't heard that my dog is dead?

"Dog is dead!" This was the key phrase of Schraeling's "late" philosophy. Soon it was being debated in beer halls and salons all across Germany. There was little discussion among Schraeling's colleagues in the philosophical profession, however. Many of them openly declared that Schraeling had abandoned philosophy altogether.

Zalmoxis is a challenging work, but it is false to say that it is not a work of philosophy. In the later portions, after one has got past the thinly disguised allegory on the Napoleonic code (*die verkehrte Eier*), the eggnog recipe, and the passionate plea on behalf of ear candling, one comes to the explicitly metaphysical sections. To be sure, these are put in the mouth of an idiot named "Stinking Simon," but most scholars now agree that Stinking Simon speaks for Schraeling (and that the "Simon" in question is Simon Magus, whose thoughts on curing leather were greatly valued by Schraeling). In this section, called "Simon Says," Schraeling outlines a metaphysics in which all of reality is seen as a reflection of an infinite, striving Odor (*das Geschmell*). In a return to a type of thinking characteristic of the pre-Socratics, Schraeling asserts that at root, all things are this Odor, and that "it stinks" (*es stinkt*).

It is at this precise point that the two streams of Schraelingians have their origin. The Classical School takes Schraeling's words literally, as metaphysics. On the other hand, the Existential Schraelingians interpret "it stinks" as figurative. They see him as a precursor to Sartre. From an examination of Schraeling's *Nachlass*, however, it seems clear that he means us to take his words literally.

"Odor," Schraeling says, rarefies and condenses to form the things of this world. We do not notice it in its pure form because we are too used to smelling it. We would only notice its absence, if that were possible. Sometimes, in a diffuse form, Odor lingers, causing Angst, and what Schraeling calls the Stale (or, in the original notes to *Zalmoxis*, the "Struggle Unto Breath"). Borrowing a term from Aristotle, Schraeling calls man's intellect *nous*, and declares that it is rarefied Odor. Life is a process of perfecting the Odor immanent within the individual. In passages clearly influenced by alchemical ideas, he distinguishes four "colors" (or, in the notes, "humors") of Odor. The last stage, associated—in Kundalini fashion—with the tip of the nose, Schraeling describes as "a kind of sweet, Honeysuckle sort of odor." In short, man's task on earth is to "perfect" Being by raising its "stuff" from stench to perfume. However, Schraeling sounds a pessimistic note at the end of *Zalmoxis*, when he declares that, ultimately, this is impossible, and that we must instead "wait for rain."

The day after his seventieth birthday, Schraeling was out walking on the Kurfürstendamm, and saw a man stomping on a beetle. Schraeling flung himself onto the insect and began trying to give it the kiss of life. When it was apparent that the creature would not survive, Schraeling began weeping and wailing uncontrollably. A crowd formed, but no one recognized him as the great Professor Schraeling. He was arrested, straitjacketed, and locked up in the city's mad house. Three days passed before Ursula learned of his incarceration. The rector of the university persuaded the authorities to release Schraeling and to send him home into the care of his wife. There, surrounded by family and friends, he was able to recover his composure, but Schraeling was never the same again. He never wrote another philosophical work, and was incapable of lecturing.

Schraeling spent his last days at the pianoforte, beating it with a large mallet. When the instrument was removed, Schraeling beat his head against the wall until the piano was put back.

Ursula suffered patiently through this, and still worse behavior. Her pain is apparent in one of her letters to her sister, Gertude:

> When he is not abusing the pianoforte, he sits on the chamber pot, shouting down at his privy parts. The cat has abandoned us, after Karl-Heinz tried to train it as a valet. Then there was the awful business with the neighbor's washing. I had no idea it had always fascinated him so. The leeching seemed to remove some of his obsession, however, just as the doctor had predicted. We received another case of vinegar today. Apparently, Karl-Heinz orders them when I am out. One has to watch him like a hawk. The other day I caught him trying to add footnotes to a large slice of roast beef. Madness does not run in his family. What can have caused this? We fear it may be the air here. My cousin Otto, who is a physician, recommends he take the cure at a spa. But I am skeptical. My father took the cure and twenty-three years later he was dead.

For five years, Schraeling lingered on in this fashion. Then, one evening, he entered the sitting room clutching at his stomach. "I have the most terrible pains in my head," he said, and collapsed. The family doctor pronounced it a case of acute, undefined discomfort of unknown origin. On his deathbed, Schraeling asked that his body be mummified, and that whoever replaced him in his chair at the university be compelled to sleep with the mummy on the third Wednesday of each month. Then came his final words: "Even I have not understood me."

Yes, Heidegger had read Schraeling long ago, but so far had avoided lecturing on him. "Climacus, I think it's time you had your dinner," Jackson said, playing with Heidegger's ear. "Then, after that, would you like a bubble bath?"

An hour later, Heidegger was in Jackson's bedroom. The plate in front of him was now clean, except for a few crumbs. He was finishing his Warsteiner. The featureless, steel door hissed open and Jackson entered, wearing what appeared to be a fluorescent green doorman's uniform. "All done? I've got something else you might like to drink." One of the clowns entered, carrying a tray. On it were two tin cans, with the tops popped. One was Mountain Dew, the other Dr. Pepper. The clown set the tray down on the bed in front of Heidegger. Jackson indicated the Mountain Dew can. "This is Jesus juice." He indicated the other can. "That's Jesus blood. Try some. Try both." Curious, Heidegger lifted the can of Mountain Dew and sipped. It was obviously a cheap, sweet, Rhine wine.

He tried the other. Probably merlot. Jackson had inched forward a bit. "Are you feeling sleepy?"

Suddenly, a hidden alarm went off, at ear-splitting volume. A large TV monitor dropped down from a hidden recess in the ceiling, showing a black and white image of the courtyard outside the house. Two cars had pulled into the circular driveway. Both were unusually tiny, with rounded tops. They looked like caricatures of Volkswagens. Their doors opened, and figures came tumbling out. At first there was too much confusion for Heidegger to make out who—or what—had arrived. But then suddenly the picture was clear to him: the courtyard was swarming with dozens of clowns. Clown after clown streamed out of the two cars. They scattered in all directions, and they were all carrying large, grey objects.

"Oh, no!" cried Jackson.

Suddenly, the clown who had brought in the tray reached into his baggy, polka-dotted trousers and pulled out a Glock. "Get your hands up, Jackson!" he cried.

"Are you . . . are you the police?"

The clown laughed malevolently. "Afraid you've been caught with your hands in the cookie jar?"

Jackson thrust his hands toward the ceiling and gasped. "What do you want?"

All at once there was a deafening CRACK! And the smell of gunpowder filled the air. Blood spurted from the clown's neck, and he collapsed to the plush, royal blue carpet. Bertha Kittridge stood in the doorway, behind the smoking barrel of a Luger. She stepped forward and approached the shaken Jackson. "The clowns have already penetrated the security in the Imagination Wing. It's only a matter of time before they locate the private quarters. I've prepared your bathosub."

But Jackson just carried on whimpering and rubbing his hands together. "Mr. Jackson!" cried Kittridge. "Pull yourself together. Think of our work. We must get you and all of our records to safety."

"Yes, yes you're right. But what about him . . . ?" He pointed to Heidegger, who was peeping out from under the bed.

"Leave it to me, Mr. Jackson. Quickly now, get down the laundry shoot. Wurlitzer will strap you into the bathosub." Jackson disappeared down the corridor, flailing his arms.

Kittridge leveled the Luger at Heidegger's brow. "Goodbye, Cliotus."

Heidegger in Chicago

"But the agon! The nobility of the agon!"

CHAPTER THREE

"Vegas"

Dear Professor Heidegger,

My name is Peter Badgerhead. I am writing you this letter because I genuinely believe that you may be the only person in the world who can understand my problem. I live in Las Vegas with my mother. She works as a cashier at the Casino Deluxe. She's been there forty years. My father abandoned us when I was eight and neither of us has ever seen him since. I work in Slot Machine, a local adult bookstore. We've got these video booths in the back. My job is to go in there with a mop every so often and clean them out. I'm also supposed to yell at guys if they're loitering around too much. But I don't like to do that. I have a problem with assertiveness. My high school guidance counselor said I was conflict adverse, whatever that means. Anyway, I live in Mom's basement. I'm thinking about maybe trying to go to graduate school in philosophy. I got a degree in philosophy from the local community college. I had this Professor there named Stan Earwig. Have you ever heard of him? He published the response to the Gettier problem in the February 1965 issue of *Dialogue*. Anyway, he said I was one of the best students to come through there in years.

But I digress. What I need to know from you is have you seen the Zapruder film? You have to be careful because sometimes when you see the film it's been cut. Like sometimes they cut the frames where you can see our dear President Kennedy's head explode (God rest his soul). Anyway, there's a certain point at which the film jumps and something seems to go in front of the camera. Do you remember that? I think the film may have been tampered with. Maybe something's been cut that they don't know want us to see.

So I heard you're coming to Vegas to give a lecture. I was wondering if I could possibly meet with you. If necessary, I could show you the Zapruder film and then get your opinion. Would that be okay?

I just want you to know that I don't believe all that talk about you being a Nazi. I've learned so much about being from your books. I mean, it's been such a revelation to me. I've learned a whole

new way of life from *Being and Time*.
I was wondering, can I have a video of you chopping wood?

Sincerely,
Peter Badgerhead

Heidegger set the letter down with a weary sigh. He had received so many letters about the Zapruder film. The previous summer, at the hut in Todtnauberg, he had set pen to paper and had begun an essay, "The Clearing in the Grassy Knoll," an analysis of the meaning of the Kennedy assassination, in terms of the history of Being.

The concierge at the Sands had delivered this particular letter to him. It was written in a childish hand. A school essay had been enclosed, "A Report on Heidegger's *Being and Time*, for Professor Earwig's Phil 217-A, Living Issues in Existential Philosophy, by Peter Badgerhead, SS# 197-455-2134."

Heidegger glanced at the first page and was astonished to find that the paper was not only compellingly written, but that it reflected a profound understanding of his ideas. Page three contained a criticism of the concept of Care which Heidegger had never considered.

He picked up the letter again. At the bottom was a telephone number. Heidegger made it a point never to become personally involved with his fans, but something about this individual strangely intrigued him.

Against his better judgment, he found himself reaching for the telephone.

But wait! There was that lunch planned for today. When was it? 1:30. And it was 12:30 now. He still had to shower and change his clothes. Heidegger resolved to call Badgerhead after lunch, if at all. He tucked the letter into the pocket of his suit jacket, which he had laid out on the bed.

A half hour later Heidegger was in a taxi headed across town. He pressed his nose to the window and gasped. Las Vegas was uglier than he had ever imagined it could be. A vast, gaudy junkyard of casinos and strip joints, all fronted by tasteless, gilt-edged facades and enormous signs announcing the names of vulgar entertainers. He shuddered at the thought of those signs lit up by night, and made a mental note that he would not go out after dark.

Heidegger sat back in his seat and reflected on the events of the preceding three days. He looked down at the scratch on the back of his right hand and remembered his struggle with Jackson in the octopus grotto beneath Neverland Ranch. It had been the Contessa Chinchilla Heatherton at the head of the invading army of clowns. Tyler Hassenpfeffer had caught the Berrys kidnapping Heidegger on videotape and, at Chinchilla's insistence, turned it over to the Special Operations unit of the Academy of Motion Picture Arts and Sciences. In a secret lab in Santa Monica, technicians from Industrial

Light and Magic had blown up stills from the film and used a sophisticated face recognition program to identify the Berrys, who were both ex-cons. Two months earlier, the Berrys (calling themselves the Dickersons) had been slapped with a restraining order, ordering them to stay away from Moehl Jackson. It didn't take much to figure out that the Berrys were headed toward Neverland Ranch and were trying to pass Heidegger off as their child.

In a matter of hours, Chinchilla, using her old TV connections, had assembled several dozen seasoned stuntmen, outfitted with clown costumes, so that they would blend in with Jackson's servants. But these were no ordinary clown costumes. The wardrobe department at Eon Productions had fitted each costume with two concealed shoulder holsters. Some of the polka dots were detachable and, when crumpled and thrown, would explode on impact. The clowns' red noses were molded from a powerful plastic explosive. Their huge clown shoes were balanced for throwing. Each clown carried a seltzer bottle in a side pocket, containing a nerve agent. Each was also issued a bicycle horn. When the bulb was squeezed, the horn functioned as a blunderbuss, and would blast a cloud of grapeshot. Hand buzzers were rigged to deliver a 1,700 volt shock, whoopee cushions were filled with sarin gas, and the fake dog poop was real.

Academy Award Winning cinematographer Joe Birock, A.S.C., had put the security cameras around Neverland out of commission, and a pyrotechnics team from M-G-M had blasted the front gates. At precisely 9:00pm, the raiding party had entered the grounds of the ranch—just at the point when Heidegger was being offered the Jesus juice.

When Bertha Kittridge had leveled her Luger at Heidegger, the philosopher thought he had had it. But milliseconds later, Bertha had screamed in agony as a stiletto-tipped clown shoe sunk into her brain. It had been thrown—expertly—by Hop Theng, Chinchilla's Korean manservant. Chinchilla herself, dressed in a chic, black clown suit from Givenchy had rushed into the bedroom, tears streaming through her makeup, and had embraced Heidegger. Meanwhile, the rescue party were involved in a fierce gun battle with Jackson's men. Heidegger changed channels on the closed circuit monitor and they were able to watch the melee, as armed clowns battled it out from behind the huge lollipops in the Imaginarie. On another monitor, they were horrified to see that Jackson, apparently using a remote control device, had opened the cages in the bestiary and unleashed the animals. In the foreground of the picture, they could see a great python with an enormous bulge in its gullet. Two absurdly long clown shoes poked out from its jaws. "Moment!" Hop Theng had cried, and he pressed a button which caused the closed circuit camera to pan across the bestiary. At the very back, they could see the glass case containing Karl-Heinz Rudiger Gunther Schraeling's mummy *rising* out of the floor.

Da haben wir es ja, was wir wollen! thought Heidegger, and he led Chinchilla down the corridor, into the elevator, down three flights, and through a back way into the bestiary. They encountered minimal resistance. Just as they entered the bestiary, a giant vampire bat had swooped down and almost become entangled in Chinchilla's hair. Heidegger quickly calmed her. When they came to the case containing Schraeling's mummy, it took Heidegger only a few seconds to find the way to open it. The three of them now stepped inside and huddled close to the ghastly corpse. As soon as they shut the glass door behind them, the case began descending into the floor. Slowly, they went down, down into the subterranean depths of Neverland, through a featureless shaft of concrete. At last, the case BUMPED to a stop at the bottom of a large cave lit by floodlights. At its center was a man-made lagoon, and a long channel leading out, presumably into the ocean. Heidegger saw Jackson and Kittridge—still alive! Somehow she had gotten past the trio and joined Jackson. The clown shoe was still stuck in her head. The two of them were huddled over an object that looked rather like a huge, plastic thermos: Jackson's personal submarine.

Heidegger opened the glass case as quietly as he could, and the three crept forward. Kittridge was opening the hatch of the bathosub, telling Jackson to get in without delay. Heidegger had to act fast. Crouching behind some boulders, he began reciting Hölderlin in a loud voice. Kittridge swung around, gun drawn, in time for her chin to connect with Hop Theng's left heel. He had given her a vicious savate kick, and the impact sent the gun flying out of her hand, and clattering to Jackson's feet. Jackson recoiled from it as if it were a deadly snake. Chinchilla, Heidegger, and Jackson now watched in silence as a spectacular display of martial arts unfolded before them. Kittridge and Hop Theng traded blows, any one of which would have killed an ordinary human being. From somewhere, Kittridge produced a trident, but Hop Theng chopped the wooden handle in two with the side of his hand, and the pieces splashed into the lagoon. Just when it seemed Hop Theng had the upper hand, Kittridge gave him a nasty chop in the groin. The little manservant doubled over in pain, but as Kittridge bent down to strangle him with her bare hands, Hop Theng suddenly whirled around and yanked the stiletto-tipped clown show from her cranium. The effect was remarkable. Kittridge simply froze. She stayed locked in the same position—bent over, reaching for Hop

Theng. Even her eyelids stayed fixed, unblinking. Heidegger, Chinchilla, and Hop Theng contemplated this macabre spectacle for a few moments, and then turned just in time to see Jackson disappearing into his bathosub. With a ROAR of exhaust, he activated the atomic batteries. A tsunami of lagoon water now washed up and over the heroic trio, as the bathosub disappeared down the channel.

Heidegger had declined lunch with the president of Columbia Pictures, who wanted to present him with the Order of Bumstead. The studio writers' department had told Heidegger that they were pretty sure Jackson could have somehow used his bone marrow extraction process to create an army of super beings. Intending to head off to an undisclosed location for a little R&R, Heidegger and Chinchilla booked a sleeping car on the 20th Century. It was obvious to Heidegger that the woman was infatuated with him, and there, in the sleeping car, in gratitude for rescuing him, he had given her what she wanted. After spending a couple of days together, however, Heidegger had wearied of her company. After a tearful goodbye, he caught a flight to Vegas.

The cab now stopped outside a short, squat brick structure, built in a "fabulous fifties" style. An oval sign on an outcrop of brick read "SANTORI'S RESTAURANT." Heidegger paid the driver, got out, and entered the building. He was surprised to find the large, dimly lit dining room almost empty of patrons. Its rich, dark wood paneling only added to the gloom. When Heidegger spoke his name to the maitre d', the man, an elderly Italian, practically genuflected, and quickly escorted him to a round booth at the very back of the restaurant. A man was already seated there, smoking a cigarette. He wore a raincoat, draped casually over one shoulder, and sported a small hat, of a type that had often been worn by men twenty years earlier, but had long since gone out of fashion.

"Professor Heidegger!" the man drawled loudly. "Have a seat. I'm Milo Artanis."

Yes, even Heidegger knew that name. The legendary singer. The great "crooner" of the 1940s. The Vegas entertainer. The film star. The reputed mob favorite.

"Can I get you a drink?" Artanis asked. Before Heidegger could answer, he swiveled his head toward the front of the room and bellowed, "Arty! A scotch and soda for my friend here, and another one for me too."

"Right away, Mr. Artanis," a faint voice called back.

"Did you have a good trip? Are they treating you alright at the Sands? Because . . ." and now he leaned in close to Heidegger and jabbed the tablecloth with his index finger. ". . . if they're not you just tell me. Tell ME, see? Because I've got connections. I can fix you up."

Heidegger indicated that he was finding

"Vegas"

his accommodations quite adequate. The elderly maitre d', who apparently did double duty as a waiter, brought the two drinks and took their order. "I'll have the veal," Artanis said. The waiter smiled. Obviously, this was Artanis's "usual." The singer turned to Heidegger. "I recommend the veal. Really. It's the best thing on their menu. He'll have the veal," he said to the waiter, who then departed swiftly.

Artanis removed a fresh cigarette from a gold plated case and lit up. "So, to come to the point, Professor. You don't mind if I call you Marty, do you? So anyway, to come to the point, I need your stuff."

Heidegger stared into his blue eyes, uncomprehending.

"You're the next big thing! You ARE the big thing! Your whole philosophy, all that jazz, it's sweeping the fuckin' country. And after that business with Jackson—Jesus, what a perv!—you're a national—no, an international hero! So, I need your stuff." Seeing that Heidegger still did not understand, he learned forward and became more excited. "Your material . . . Your words. I got this music man, Kurt Kataract. You heard of him? Everybody has. He's going to put your words to music. I figured we could start with 'The Origin of the Work of Art.' Or maybe 'The Question Concerning Technology.' What do you think?"

Heidegger was speechless.

"Listen, if it's a question of, well . . . you

know . . ." Artanis was rubbing his thumb and index finger together. "Don't worry about that. I'm going to get you a fantastic deal."

The front door opened abruptly, casting a long rectangle of light over the shadowy room. A tall, thin man had entered and was approaching. He was young, but his hair was white. He wore a navy blue turtleneck, and a peace medallion dangled around his chest. "Kurt, baby!" Artanis called out. The two men greeted each other warmly, and then Heidegger was introduced to the newcomer, who turned out to be the aforementioned Kurt Kataract. "Listen, Marty. Kurt here is going to sit down at the piano and we'll do a little demo for you. Just the stuff we've worked out so far." There was a baby grand across the room. Artanis motioned for Heidegger to relocate himself, and the philosopher complied, sitting down at a table quite close to the piano. Kataract now sat before the instrument, and Artanis stood next to him. "Now you understand, this is pretty rough. But it'll give you a good idea."

Kataract began playing the opening bars of a jaunty melody. After a few notes, he said "This is where the horns'll come in."

"Okay, okay. Save it kid," Artanis said. "Just let me do the driving." Now he threw his head back and began to sing.

Only image formed keeps the viSION!
    YET—image formed rests in the po-

"Vegas"

> EM!
> (Artanis was snapping his fingers at
> this point.)
> How could cheerfullness stream
> through US if we wanted to shun
> sadNUSS?!
> Oh, yeah . . . !
> Pain gives of its healing power where
> we least EX-PECT it!
> Scooby dooby doo . . .

Heidegger sat with his hands folded in his lap, unsure of what to make of this. He did not immediately recognize the words as his own, but when he did he felt a sinking sensation and looked away.

"What'd ya think, Doc?" Kataract asked.

Before Heidegger could answer, Artanis cut in. "Don't bother the man, Kurt! He's a thinker. He's a thinker. Give him time. Let's do another number. One. Two. ONE—TWO—THREE—FOUR . . . !"

> We never come to thoughts. They come
> to ussssssss . . .
> THAT is the proper hour of discourse!
> Discourse cheers us to companionable reflecSHUN!
> Such reflection neither parades polem .
> . . .

Artanis stumbled over ". . . polemical opinions"

. . . nor does it tolerate complaisant agreement. The sail of thinking . . .'

"Jesus! We're going to have to hire Marilyn and Alan Bergman to smooth this stuff out."

The front door opened again. None of them heard it, but another long rectangle of light spread out slowly across the floor. They all turned to look. In walked a middle-aged man of average height, balding on top, and dressed entirely in black.

"Jesus Christ it's the A.P.A.," Artanis whispered.

The man walked slowly toward them. He took a cigarette from a pack in his coat pocket and lit it with what looked like a large, old fashioned tabletop lighter. It made a loud CLICK as he popped open the top and shut it again. "Hello boys," he said.

Artanis stepped forward. "May I introduce you gentlemen? Marty, Kurt, this is Robert Q. DeNameland, Consigliere to the Vegas chapter of the American Philosophical Association," he made the introduction in an exaggeratedly formal, ironic manner. "Professor DeNameland, this . . ."

"Yeah, I know who he is," DeNameland rasped. He meant Heidegger. Kataract didn't exist, as far as he was concerned. He took a long drag on the cigarette. "Looks like you boys have got quite a party goin' here. Mind if I join in?"

Artanis hesitated. "Sure," he said. "We

were just letting Professor Heidegger hear some of our material."

DeNameland pulled a chair out from a nearby table and straddled it, the chair back to his chest. "Well, I'd LOVE to hear some too. Play on McDuff."

Artanis nodded to Kataract, who looked worried, then cleared his throat and began again.

> The world's darkening never reaches to
> the light of Being . . .
> We are too late for the gods and too
> early for BEEEing!
> Being's poem, JUST beguuuuuun . . .
> is MAN!

"Wait! Wait! Wait a minute!" DeNameland called out, interrupting them. Artanis and Kararact stopped abruptly. "Those is philosophical lyrics, ain't they?"

"Well . . . I suppose . . . you could call them that," Artanis stammered.

"Yeah, I COULD call them that, cause they are. You know the score, Milo. If you're gonna play it in Vegas, then . . ."

"I know that, Bobby. But this isn't for Vegas it's for my new album. It's national. I'm gonna record the songs in New York." Artanis was sweating.

"New York? I'll have to let the Eastern Division know about this."

The front door opened again—but this time so violently that it BANGED against the wall of the foyer. A tall, thin man entered and moved quickly towards them. He was wearing a short-sleeve, white dress shirt from which a black pocket protector stuck out awkwardly. The man put his hands on his hips. "What's going on here?" he said.

"Easy, Milt. We're just havin' a little concert," DeNameland drawled, without getting up.

"Well, the word on the street is that they're philosophical songs he's playin' here."

"So what if they are. There's no harm in that," DeNameland answered. He turned to Heidegger. "You'll have to forgive my colleague here. We sort of . . . co-run the Vegas A.P.A. We represent the two families, if you will."

"I want to hear this stuff, Bobby," Milt Dedwood said, threateningly.

Artanis stretched his arms out in a peacemaking gesture. "Relax, boys. I'll just play another one."

> When thought's courage stems from the bidding of BEEEing, then DEStiny's language thrives . . .
> As soon as we have the thing before our eyes, and in our hearts an ear for the woooooord . . .
> Thinking prospers . . .
> She-bop! She-bop!

There was a long silence after Artanis finished. Dedwood was shaking his head, his lower lip quivering. "I think I heard wrong. That don't sound like philosophy to me. No sir." He turned and marched out, letting the door SLAM behind him.

"Fuckin' analytic philosopher!" DeNameland called after him. "Sorry for that rude interruption, gentlemen. Did you know that the average analytic journal article contains close to 2% mouse parts? Anyway, back to business Milo. And I don't appreciate being given the runaround."

As Artanis and DeNameland continued arguing it out, Heidegger rose slowly and looked around for the WC.

"Hey, where d'ya think you're going?!" DeNameland called out, but he quickly corrected himself: "I mean, can I help you with something Professor Heidegger?"

Heidegger indicated that he only wanted to use the restroom and would be back in a moment. Artanis told him to turn the corner nearest them. He would find the restroom at the end of the corridor. As Heidegger went on his way, he glanced in the direction of the front window, which was covered by partially closed Venetian blinds. He saw two black sedans parked out front. Four men, all dressed in dark suits and wearing sunglasses, were loitering around the sedans, smoking cigarettes. Heidegger was getting a terrible feeling about this whole situation. A range of possibilities flashed through his mind. Could he crawl out the bathroom window? Or exit via the kitchen? He might get out of the building, but he was a celebrity. The men in black could spot him before he got very far. And where else might they be stationed? No, he needed a getaway.

Heidegger entered the bathroom. There was a window large enough for a man to crawl through, just above the toilet. He opened it as gingerly as he could. He saw an alleyway outside, and a street sign. Good, at least he knew his approximate location. But who could provide him with aid? Heidegger reached into his jacket pocket to retrieve his handkerchief, but instead pulled out a folded envelope. It was the letter from Peter Badgerhead. Heidegger opened it. Yes, the phone number was scrawled at the bottom, just as he had thought it was. Heidegger had passed a pay phone in the corridor, on the way to the bathroom. As quietly as he could, he stepped back out into the corridor, easing the door closed. He could hear the three men in the dining room, arguing violently. Heidegger fumbled with the unfamiliar American change in his pocket, and put a handful of it into the pay phone. Several of the coins came jingling down into the coin return slot. Heidegger waited for any sign that the men had heard, but none came. He dialed Peter Badgerhead's phone number.

There were four rings, then the receiver was lifted. "Hello?" said a quavering male voice. Heidegger began to introduce himself, as quietly as he could while still remaining audible. He heard a woman calling out in the background. "Just a minute, ma!" the man said. "Now what did you say your name was?" Heidegger introduced himself and was about to explain his situation, but was cut off. "Professor Heidegger! This is Peter Badgerhead! Oh, Jeez! Oh my gosh! I didn't think when I wrote down . . . Golly! I can't believe . . . I mean, like, you're my IDOL. I worship you. I . . ." Heidegger cut in and explained his situation. He had to do this three times until he was fairly confident Badgerhead had understood him, and then he made his request. "The corner of . . . Sure! Sure!" Badgerhead cried, "I don't live too far. I could be there in maybe fifteen minutes. No, make it ten! I'll be there in five! Just stop at the alleyway? Okay, but a distinguished man like you . . . Oh, right. I'll shut up now. Okay, you can count on me Professor Heidegger! I'll see you then. Goodbye Professor Heidegger." And the phone went dead.

Heidegger now went back into the bathroom and eased the window open. He sat on the sill, drew his knees up, and swiveled out and over into the alleyway, then hopped down. Heidegger was quite pleased with himself. He was more agile than he thought he would be. Quickly, he made for the entrance to the alley. Looking to his right, he could see the front fender of one of the sedans. Suddenly, one of the black-clothed men appeared. He tossed a spent cigarette onto the pavement and crushed it with the toe of his shoe, then turned about and disappeared. Heidegger ducked back into the alleyway. He remembered that he had not thought to ask Badgerhead what kind of car he would be driving. Still, he had given his location in very explicit terms, and he was sure Badgerhead would recognize him from the many photographs printed on the dust jackets of his books.

Heidegger looked at his watch. He figured he had been standing in the alley close to five minutes now. Suddenly, with a screech, a banana yellow Volkswagen Rabbit lurched up directly in front of him. A round, cherubic face beamed at him from the interior, beckoning him to get in. Heidegger did so, and they sped right past the men in black, who noticed nothing.

Heidegger sat back and sighed in relief.

"Boy, I sure am honored to meet you, Professor Heidegger. I mean, I just can't believe this is happening. Why did you decide to call me?" The man said it as if he couldn't imagine *anyone* deciding to call him. Heidegger reminded him of his situation. "Yeah," Badgerhead said, "You gotta watch out for those A.P.A. guys in Vegas. They're a different breed out here. Really rough. Although it's been better since the truce."

Heidegger asked him what he meant.

"The truce between the analysts and the pluralists. Boy, before that things were really bad. They would break up each other's

"Vegas"

colloquia, there were death threats, everything. The final straw was when the pluralists invited Derrida to town. Three goons from the analytic wing—a logician, a philosopher of mind, and an ethicist—they did a drive-by. Nobody was hurt, but Derrida did get hit with some flying glass. After that was when they decided they'd better make some kind of a deal. I mean, if a kid took classes from analytic philosophers and then tried to take a class on Husserl, a couple of enforcers—usually logicians—would come over, break some of his bones. One time they carved an existential quantifier on some poor guy's ass. I got beat up once by a philosopher of language. He kept knocking me in the head and saying 'Clear? Is it clear to you what I'm saying?' But I couldn't retain all the abbreviations he was using, so I kept saying no, and he just kept hitting me. But the pluralists aren't any better. In fact in some ways they're worse. They'll talk to you about tolerance and academic freedom while they're putting your head in a vice or braining you with a baseball bat. But most of what they say you can't even understand. Even Derrida was freaked out by them. So where are we going, Professor Heidegger?"

Heidegger suggested that Badgerhead drop him back at the Sands, but Badgerhead didn't think that was such a good idea. "That's just where they're expecting you to go. Trust me, you've crossed 'em now, and they don't like that. You go back to your hotel room, and there are gonna be a couple of deconstructionists there with a blowtorch and a pair of pliers. You need a place to hide out for a while, and I know just the place."

A few minutes later they were pulling into a rather seedy housing development called Rancho Notorious. As soon as Heidegger got out of the car, he was hit with the thudding bass of "rap music."

"This way, Professor. This way." Badgerhead escorted him to a lower level apartment in one of the buildings. Heidegger caught the scent of boiling cabbage before Badgerhead had even opened the door. "Home sweet home!" he cried. "Mom! I've brought you a visitor!" Heidegger heard the call of a bird, probably a cockatoo, and the muffled voice of an older woman, obviously protesting having a guest thrust on her without warning. The apartment was clearly the mother's. Every furnishing, every last touch was that of the Little Old Lady, right down to the lace doilies on the arms of the chairs. Heidegger felt that he was suffocating. He loosened his tie, just as Badgerhead reappeared with a tray of drinks. "I thought you might be a little thirsty after your ordeal. I mean, after what happened. So I brought you some Seven Up." Heidegger took the glass with a polite gesture of thanks. "So, would you like to meet Mom?"

Badgerhead guided Heidegger down a short corridor and toward his mother's bedroom. He turned quickly and whispered,

"Vegas"

"Mom's a bit of a handful."

The mother's bedroom was dominated by a huge, brass bed, and the bed was dominated by the largest woman Heidegger had ever seen. It looked as if her great bulk had been poured into the mattress. It was not clear where she ended and the blankets and stuffing began. "Hey, honey," the woman barked suspiciously after Badgerhead's elaborate introduction. Heidegger bowed. It was a wonder the woman could talk at all. The triple rings of fat that were her neck looked like they ought to choke off speech. Heidegger noticed that beside her was a large paper bucket of fried chicken parts. Mrs. Badgerhead picked up a drumstick and began gnawing on it.

"I left Mom her dinner before I came to get you," Badgerhead explained. "The cabbage is for me. For later."

"So, what the fuck are you?" Mrs. Badgerhead exclaimed, her mouth full of fowl.

"Mom, really!"

Heidegger explained calmly that he was a philosopher.

"Yeah," she drawled. "Bunch of horseshit if you ask me."

Badgerhead drew himself up. "Mom, I've been telling you for years. Philosophy is the oldest and noblest of all the disciplines. Why . . . it asks fundamental questions that help guide our life. And the agon! The nobility of the agon! It enriches us, Mom."

"Yeah, that's why you're swabbing sperm

at the local jack shack." She spat a bone onto the comforter.

Badgerhead quickly bustled Heidegger out of the bedroom. "Mom's always a little grumpy before her main course," he whispered. When they had returned to the parlor, Heidegger was bidden to seat himself in a stiff, highly uncomfortable Victorian armchair.

Badgerhead stood before him, bent slightly with his hands pressed together, as if about to beg. "Uh, while we're waiting for . . . for when you can safely be on your way, I thought I might share with you some of my journals. I'll read them to you. The stuff about you is really . . . really okay, I think. I started it while I was in a . . . facility." Now he lowered his eyes. "Nothing dramatic. I just started drinking a little too much cough medicine, so Mom put me someplace for a while where they could help. Anyways, I wrote a lot in my journal about *Being and Time* while I was there. I'll go get it and read it to you." He disappeared into a little alcove and began opening drawers, hunting for the journal.

Heidegger drew his knees up to his chest and embraced them. He kept thinking to himself, *Mein Gott, Mein Gott, Mein Gott, Mein Gott, Mein Gott . . .*

"Vegas"

"Fisting? Oh, please don't get me started talking about my second husband."

CHAPTER FOUR

"San Francisco"

The lesbians of Berkeley can strip a man to the bone in thirty seconds. At least, that was what Heidegger had heard. They lumbered around the U.C. Berkeley campus, their large, pale, shapeless bodies suspended in boiler suits. Land manatees with buzzcut heads full of raised consciousness. One of them dropped a few quarters into the cup of coffee Heidegger was holding as he stood on Telegraph Avenue, trying to find his bearings. He had not been enjoying the coffee anyway.

Heidegger had flown into Oakland in the late morning, and had been picked up by his host, Furness Meeks, a professor of theology at the Berkeley Union of Liberal Learning, School of Higher Involvement in Theology, or B.U.L.L.S.H.I.T., as the locals called it. When Heidegger had exited his plane, bags in hand, he had seen Meeks standing with families waiting to greet their returning loved ones. He was bald on top, with a very long, grey beard, and wore a tee shirt and a broad grin. Meeks approached Heidegger with arms outstretched. "Martin! Welcome," he said, and embraced Heidegger. The philosopher was glad he had his hands full with his raincoat and briefcase, as he was not sure how he should respond.

In Meeks' Volkswagen van, Heidegger had asked him about his institution's curious name. "You know, Martin, it's an odd story. Originally the school was called the Hackett School of Theology. But the Hacketts were a wealthy, white family from San Francisco, and none of us really liked having that as our image. Of course, when we changed the name we lost the Hackett money, so that's why we affiliated with B.U.L.L. We had a meeting to decide on the new name. It dragged on for about fourteen hours. Various ideas were proposed. Lee, one of my best friends on the faculty, wanted to call it the School for Enlightened, Non-Racist, Non-Sexist, Non-Classist, Non-Homophobic, Non-Eurocentric, Non-Christocentric Study of Interfaith, Non-Sectarian Theology. One person objected that that was too long. But he's sort of a dinosaur, and dead now anyway. The real trouble was we couldn't agree on the word order."

Heidegger raised his eyebrows.

"I mean, Tina, who was a transgendered student in the program, argued that it was demeaning to make 'non-homophobic' the fourth adjective on the list, as if it's the fourth most important issue. Everyone was prepared to give in to him . . . *er* . . . her and make it item number two, but then Pat Smear, who is a very prominent feminist scholar on our faculty, objected that 'non-sexist' absolutely had to stay where it was. Anyway, that whole discussion actually took place at the second meeting, which lasted thirty-six hours. But we couldn't reach any agreement. So 'School of Higher Involvement in Theology' was kind of a compromise name. We worked that one out over the course of a third meeting, during which that older professor—the one I said was a dinosaur—during which he passed away."

Heidegger asked why the words "higher involvement in theology" had been chosen.

Meeks laughed uncomfortably, as if caught out in an embarrassing mistake. "Well, it's a little too specific, I know. But we wanted to convey the idea that our program is a place where students come to learn about diversity, and to become involved in meaningful activities that promote diversity, and that combat racism, sexism, homophobia, and ethnocentrism. The students and the faculty work on community outreach programs dealing with multiculturalism. We work with the homeless, we campaign for progressive politicians, and we run a free AIDS screening clinic."

Heidegger asked if the students had any time left over to study theology.

Meeks was silent for a while. "We do some of that, yes. More recent work, of course, because the older stuff is really out of date and filled with sexist God talk."

Heidegger was scheduled to speak at B.U.L.L.S.H.I.T.'s Interfaith Chapel that evening at 7:00 p.m. He had lunch with Meeks, but asked to be left alone to explore Berkeley by himself for the rest of the day. Somewhat disappointed, Meeks extracted from Heidegger a promise that on the following day they would do some sight-seeing together.

So now, some hours later, Heidegger stood on Telegraph Avenue, looking for the way back to the U.C. Berkeley campus. It was just after 5:00 p.m. and Heidegger was thinking about heading back toward B.U.L.L.S.H.I.T., whose campus lay on the other side of U.C. Berkeley on a hill that, provided the day was clear, afforded a magnificent view of the San Francisco Bay. Unfortunately, somehow he had gotten turned around, and could not find his way back.

Heidegger entered a bookstore called Moe's, intending simply to ask for directions, but instead he succumbed to a curious temptation. He asked where the philosophy books were, and, climbing some stairs, found a large collection of them on an upper floor. His eyes scanned the "H" section, going past Hegel, and then lighting on his own name. Almost half a shelf was taken up by English translations of Heidegger's works. He took a copy of *Basic Problems of Phenomenology* off the shelf and opened it, recoiling from the book at once, for almost every page had been defaced by a yellow highlighter pen. In some places, the yellow ink had turned a kind of burnt brown color. He was about to close the volume in disgust, when suddenly his thumb slipped and the book flipped open to the very back. On the blank pages at the back of the book, the previous owner had written, in pencil, a list of numbered items in a small, neat hand:

1. Oaxacan animals
2. New Zappa release
3. New cap
4. Kimchee

Stranger things were written in the back of this book, however. On the lower, right hand corner of one page, the book's previous owner had written, "The Duke and Duchess of Windsor."

Suddenly, Heidegger heard a man's voice call out behind him. It was high-pitched, with an English accent: "But Pookie Deamus!"

"Shut up, David!" barked a woman with a rather deep voice.

Instinctively, Heidegger snapped the book shut just as the woman rounded the corner. She was over fifty and smartly dressed, but with a harsh, angular face; not pretty in the least, but elegant. She held two pug dogs on a leash. The woman addressed herself to Heidegger. "Excuse me, do you know where the chief jeweler is?"

Heidegger hesitated, then explained that

this was a bookstore.

"You see, David. There's nothing but books here," she called behind her. "And you know my allergies. We'll have to leave."

"No!" the little man piped. He remained on the other side of one of the book cases and did not come around to speak to her. "I want to look at the golfing books."

"David . . ." she began, threateningly.

"No!" he piped, rather more meekly.

"Well, I'm surprised," she said, putting her hands on her hips. "For once you show a little backbone. But over nothing at all! How typical." She turned to Heidegger. "He'll abdicate a throne for me, but he won't leave a bookstore. Do you know any jewelers around here?"

Intimidated by the woman's manner, Heidegger began to stammer out an answer in the negative. But she cut him off: "Come on!" She paused long enough to deposit the two pugs with her husband, then headed down the stairs and out the door. Strangely, Heidegger felt he had no choice but to follow her.

Out on Telegraph Avenue, she turned to him. "It's all right if you don't know any jewelers. I just want to spend a little time away from him. He panics when I do that. Especially if I'm with another man. So we'll spend awhile together, okay? I'm Wallis, Duchess of Windsor," she said, sticking out a bony hand. Heidegger shook it and introduced himself. "Oh, a German? David and I just love Germans. David speaks the language fluently. So where shall we go?"

Heidegger indicated that he needed to head back to B.U.L.L.S.H.I.T. so that he could give his address. There was supposed to be some kind of service held beforehand, and Heidegger had promised to attend. So he and the Duchess began making their way across the U.C. Berkeley campus, during which she chattered away happily. "It's an attractive campus, don't you think? Although I would move *that* building . . . just a little bit to the left," she said, stopping to indicate with her hands. "Yes, about three feet. Oh, and I love those misty hills, although there's the most gawdawful concrete bunker architecture up there. Oh, and the palm trees are so lovely. They remind me of the Bahamas. So tell me, what sort of lecture are you giving?"

Heidegger intended to repeat the "What is Dwelling?" address he had given twice already at other universities, and he began to try and summarize it for her. The Duchess listened quietly, but soon she began to make a face as if she had just heard someone break wind. Her eyes began scanning the horizon, looking for almost anything to divert her. "Yes . . . uh huh . . . yes, well that sounds very interesting," she said when Heidegger had finished. "But frankly I think it's all just talk, and rather useless talk at that. No offense. Believe me, I know dwelling. The first place David and I dwelt was the Château de la Maye in Versailles. Oh, well that's if you don't count the Hotel Meurice. Then we moved on to the Château de la Cröe on Cap d'Antibes. That was really our first home. But a dwelling isn't just a box you put furniture and people in. You have to choose the furnishings—and, I might add, the people—to bring out the dwelling's natural virtues. So, for instance at the Mill . . ."

Heidegger interrupted her to explain that this was not the sort of thing he meant, but at this point they had just started up the hill to the B.U.L.L.S.H.I.T. campus and had run right into Furness Meeks. "Martin! I was getting worried. The service starts in about five minutes. Who's your friend?" The Duchess introduced herself simply as "Wallis," and Meeks did not recognize her. They went up the hill together, and the Duchess continued chatting about the furnishings in the various houses she and the Duke had lived in. When they reached the door of the Interfaith Chapel, a small, squat modernistic structure that didn't look like a church at all, one of the land manatees was waiting for them.

"Uh, Furness we're just about ready to begin," she said in a husky voice and ushered Heidegger, Meeks and the Duchess inside. They stood together for a couple of minutes making awkward conversation. Meeks noticed the jeweled flamingo-shaped brooch the Duchess wore on her Chanel jacket. "Oh my, that's pretty," he said. "Was it very expensive?"

The Duchess recoiled slightly, then replied, "Well, let's just say it's good enough to wear here." She glanced around the room. The chapel was devoid of decoration. There were about fifteen long pews, and a raised platform in the front of the room, which was supposed to suggest an altar. "Christ, what a dump!" the Duchess exclaimed, oblivious to the fact that she could be plainly heard. "I mean, I'm not particularly religious, but if you're going to do the whole church thing you can at least do it with style: stained glass and high, vaulted ceilings and incense. This place looks like traffic court."

Meeks shifted around uncomfortably. "Well, we didn't want to give the suggestion of endorsing any particular faith . . ."

"How do they do communion here?" the Duchess continued. "Take a number and wait your turn? 'Now serving Number 58, come get your body and blood!'"

"Perhaps you'd like to be seated now," Meeks whispered. There were about forty people present, and every one of their heads was now turned toward the Duchess. She sat next to Heidegger several pews back from the altar, and Meeks went to join the minister, who was a young woman with short, brown hair, standing near what passed for a pulpit.

"My God," the Duchess called out, "I haven't seen so many pale, unhealthy bodies since Patton liberated Dachau." She tapped the shoulder of the hefty, buzzcut lesbian sitting in front of her. "Excuse me, sir . . ." When the lesbian turned around, the Duchess gasped. "Oh! I thought you were a man! Wait, you are a man, aren't you? Professor Hildegard what is this, a man or a woman?"

"What do you want?" snarled the lesbian.

"I want to know how I can order something from the bar . . ."

At just that moment, the minister began. She had now donned lime green vestments ("Tacky," whispered the Duchess) and raised her arms to welcome the congregation. "Greetings! And a non-sectarian blessing be upon all of you!"

"And also on you!" most of the crowd called out in unison.

"We are gathered here this evening for a joyous occasion, to welcome new members of the School of Higher Involvement in Theology community. Please rise." Four individuals now stood up. They were one man and three women, including the lesbian in front of the Duchess. "We welcome you in a spirit of ecumenical fellowship," continued the minister. "And we urge you to become involved in the greater fellowship that is the Bay Area community. You may be seated. We also give an especial welcome to those of our community tonight who are African American, Latino/Latina, and Gay, Lesbian, and Transgendered, in the hopes that we may build bridges and mend fences together."

Heidegger in Chicago

The Duchess looked around the room and noticed that about two thirds of those present were white, and a third were Asian. "What are all these gooks doing here?" she asked *sotto voce*, though seven faces turned to glare at her.

Meeks now came to the podium. "It's my pleasure to introduce to you tonight a world-renowned philosopher, Martin Heidegger." There followed some details of Heidegger's career, including a list of his major publications, conveniently omitting some of the unpleasantness of the '30s and '40s. "His topic tonight is, 'What is Dwelling?'"

Heidegger rose and moved to the altar, removing his address from his inside coat pocket. He spoke slowly and carefully. Everything seemed to be going smoothly, but then about ten minutes into the talk there was a commotion in the back of the room. Heidegger looked up to see a tall black man, a latecomer to the gathering, standing near the Duchess, engaged in animated conversation with her. "No, I won't get up!" she cried. The man muttered something, but Heidegger did not hear him. "I'll be damned if you're sitting next to me!" the Duchess shouted and waved him away. The man didn't budge, however, and there now flowed from him a virtual glossary of profane language. Meeks rushed over to see what the problem was. "Don't you have a section for the coloreds?" the Duchess asked him. "When the Duke and I were in the Bahamas we didn't even let them through the front door!"

The crowd gasped. The burly lesbian in front of the Duchess fainted. The minister crossed herself, though she wasn't Catholic. Meeks shook with rage. "I'm afraid I'm going to have to ask you to leave!" he bleated.

"With pleasure!" the Duchess said, and rose quickly from the pew, her small Louis Vuitton handbag hooked over one wrist. "I've never seen such a collection of stunted, mealy-mouthed imbeciles in my entire life. Come along, Martin!" She motioned for Heidegger to follow her, and then disappeared out the door.

Strangely, unaccountably, just as before, Heidegger felt that he simply had to obey her. He tucked the speech back into his pocket and rushed outside to join the Duchess.

"But Martin! Professor Heidegger! Where are you going?! I didn't mean for you to leave!" Meeks cried. He waffled back and forth between outrage and solicitousness. "If this woman is a friend of yours, I didn't mean to . . . Well, that is to say I *hope* you don't share her views! . . . Just because she leaves doesn't mean that you . . . But then again, if you would associate with such a person then perhaps it's best . . ."

But neither Heidegger nor the Duchess heard him. It was growing dark outside, and the two of them started back down the hill under the palm trees, in the direction of the U.C. Berkeley campus. "Martin," she said, "first thing we'll do is fetch the Rolls from my hotel, then Sidney can drive us into the city and we'll have a hi-ho time! Jimmy Donahue showed me some marvelous spots on Castro Street. I wonder if they're still in business . . ."

Many hours later Heidegger and the Duchess of Windsor were sitting at a bar in San Francisco sipping martinis. Behind the bar were tall metal racks stacked with liquor, and behind the stacks were opaque sheets of plastic through which colored lights were projected. Every few seconds one color would fade into another: blue into green, into red, into orange, into purple, into blue again, etc. Heidegger decided that he liked the Duchess best when she was red; least when green. Yes, she was almost attractive when she was red. But the green light made her look like a witch from a children's stage production of "Hansel and Gretel."

He had no idea where they were, and only a dim idea of how many martinis he had already had. He seemed to vaguely remember a visit to Alcatraz involving a boat load of drag queens. They had already hit three bars by that point. Afterwards, the Duchess had amused herself by feeding truffles to a group of sea lions on the pier. One of the drag queens had taken them along to what Heidegger had thought to be a very low place, where queer things went on. Bashful as ever, he had kept his eyes focused on his martini glass most of the while. Yet he worked up the courage to ask the Duchess about one thing in particular he had caught a glimpse of.

"Fisting? Oh, please don't get me started talking about my second husband."

Heidegger thought it best to change the subject and, groping for a way out, asked the Duchess to tell him what her first husband was like.

"Win? Oh, he was a dreadful man. Just dreadful. When we were married he had a big house in Coronado, California. He'd had it since he was a bachelor. When we came back to it after the honeymoon, he showed me a rack of keys in the kitchen. There were about a dozen of them, and they opened all the major doors in the house. You see, this was one of his peculiarities: he liked to keep everything locked. Anyway, he told me, 'You may use any of these keys,'" the Duchess now tucked her chin in and lowered her pitch, "'*except this one.*' He meant the last one on the rack. 'That opens the attic. You may never enter that room,' he told me. Well, I said that that was just fine. And I meant it. My philosophy is live and let live. If Win had something he wanted hidden in that attic, it was fine with me. I was perfectly content to let that be his business. But every day after that he would come home from work—he was a flight instructor in the Navy—and put his hands on his big hips and say . . . ," the Duchess now dropped her pitch again, "'You have been into the attic, haven't you! Confess it, woman!' It was horrible, and I would say, 'No, I have not.' And I was being perfectly honest. Well, in any case, this happened so many times I got to think that he was positively *encouraging* me to go peek in that attic. But I never did. And it just made him madder and madder. Finally, we came to blows. Or rather, he did. It was an impossible situation. We just had to part ways. Would you like another martini?"

She finished off her drink and delicately blotted her lips with a folded paper napkin, leaving two crimson crescents on it. "You know, Martin, after this I think we ought to . . . Oh, my!" She had seen someone over Heidegger's shoulder. "It's Ron and Nancy Reagan. He's a crashing bore," she whispered, "talks nothing but politics and is so . . . ," she swallowed hard, "*wholesome.* But I'll have to say hello. Excuse me . . ." Heidegger now sat alone, staring down into his martini glass, wondering where the Duchess would drag him next, knowing he was powerless to resist. All of a sudden, he felt a presence near him. He looked up and saw Furness Meeks, the wispy hair on the sides of his head disheveled, his eyes wild.

"Well, I hope you're happy with yourself," he began. "Reverend Dworkin says we're going to have to perform an exorcism on the Interfaith Chapel before we can use it again. Yes, that's right. You're not hearing things. The whole place will have to be scrubbed from top to bottom and all the carpets and furniture replaced . . . what do you mean 'Why?'! Because of what your little friend the . . . the Countess Dracula did in there! Because of her obscene, racist rant! No one can use the building until it's been thoroughly cleansed. Dale Grout, the student who fainted, she's in intensive care, under heavy sedation. And poor Retrobatus Johnson, the African-American student your friend brutalized, he hasn't uttered a word since. Yes, he's completely mute. We've erected a tent on the quad and staffed it with counselors to care for the others who were present. And I don't want to talk about myself, but I've now gone through four of the seven classic stages exhibited by trauma victims. I'm feeling a fifth coming on right now! In fact, we're not sure that cleaning and then blessing the building is going to help at all. The memory could linger on indefinitely. We may have to tear the whole thing down. Dean Aspic, who's very sensitive about these things, thinks we should turn it into a basketball court as a gesture of reconciliation to the African American community. And, my God! If this gets out, the school's reputation may be harmed beyond repair. We may have to close the school entirely! We may have to kill ourselves!" The man was now shaking violently, and tears were streaming down his cheeks.

 Heidegger stood up and slapped him hard across the left side of his face.

Meeks was silent for a while, and began wiping the tears away. "You're right. You're right. I'm taking this far too lightly."

Heidegger asked him what time it was.

"It's almost 5:00 a.m."

Meeks scattered as soon as he saw the Duchess returning to Heidegger's side. "Let's get going, Martin. I feel like some air."

As the sun rose over the hills of San Francisco, the pair walked up Haight Street and into the notorious hippie quarter. They saw only a handful of other faces, and the entire area was unusually quiet. It was Saturday, and much too early for most people to be awake, especially in this neighborhood. The Duchess kept chattering away cheerfully. She dished about a freight car full of dirt on the Royal Family. She told him about the last time she had dined with General Franco. She gave him her predications about the rise and fall of hemlines for the next two decades. And she explained to him, in great detail, how to throw a successful dinner party. "One point—and this cannot be overstressed—is that the guests can wait for the food, but the food cannot wait for the guests. This goes double if there's a soufflé involved."

Presently, they came to a public park. At the entrance were a few scruffy youths, one of whom said something to Heidegger about "buds" as they passed by. He thought this curious, but gave it no further thought. They wound their way through the park, which was heavily wooded, and came to a large field. On the path running through it were a group of men and women dancing and beating drums. As Heidegger and the Duchess approached, a man joined the group and began playing a flute. There was no tune at all, just a beat, but the effect was somehow intoxicating. Heidegger looked around the clearing. There was a domed building nearby, with what appeared to be a carousel inside. There were white, modernistic buildings beyond the trees, on the misty hills above them, along with a tall radio tower.

"Well, why don't we sit down someplace and rest awhile?" said the Duchess. They noticed a small group of people sitting on a hill nearby and began walking up it. "I really shouldn't sit after all," she said. "I don't want the grass stains." Heidegger removed his suit coat and gallantly laid it down on the grass, inviting her to sit. "Thank you, Martin! You're such a dear," she said, and sat down on it. He plopped down beside her, and both of them surveyed the horizon and listened to the music. "It's so peaceful here," said the Duchess after several minutes. "I think the Duke would love it, if they'd let him putt his little balls around."

Sometime later, two young hippie girls with long skirts and flowers woven into their hair began moving unobtrusively through the crowd. Both of them carried small picnic baskets. One of the girls approached Heidegger and the Duchess and said, "Would you like some brownies made with ganja?"

"Yes, I'd love a little something sweet to nibble on," cried the Duchess. "We'll take four, two for each of us. Pay her, Martin." Heidegger took out his wallet and paid the girl. Twenty dollars seemed a lot for four brownies. "Peace!" the girl said after handing them the merchandise, and moved on to someone else. Heidegger took his time opening the cellophane on his first brownie, but the Duchess tore into hers and was soon devouring it.

"Oh, my! This is the best brownie I've ever tasted," she said. "I really must call that girl back and get the recipe. What did she say they were made with?"

Heidegger had to admit, as he got halfway through his, that there certainly was something magical about these brownies. In fact, after a few minutes he had quite forgotten himself, and was leaning back on his elbows, smiling up at the clouds.

"My, my!" exclaimed the Duchess as she finished off her second one. "Those were truly delicious, and I don't understand it, but I haven't felt this good since Queen Mary died!"

Heidegger laughed and scanned the horizon, thinking that he might like to retire to here. But Elfride would never stand for it. When his gaze returned to earth, he watched the joyful scene of dancing and drumming at the bottom of the hill. He saw

"San Francisco"

something new there, and threw back his head and laughed. The Duchess of Windsor had joined the crowd below and was moving among them. Her arms and legs cleaved the air, and her Chanel skirt flapped to and fro as she did the Watusi.

Heidegger in Chicago

Dagmar Ertl

CHAPTER FIVE

"New York"

The Plaza Hotel in Manhattan was just as Heidegger remembered it. He arrived late in the afternoon, and it was raining. The following evening, he was scheduled to make his next public appearance. It was to be held at the famous Cooper Union, and had been co-sponsored by the Rensselaer Lasch Institute and the New York University Students of Atomic Realism. Heidegger had never heard of either. The night before the event, he had been called by Brenda Lasch, apparently the wife of Rensselaer, to inform him of the arrangements. Heidegger was horrified to discover that he had inadvertently agreed to a public debate. His opponent was to be this Mr. Lasch, of whom Heidegger had also never heard. But he decided it was too late to back out at this point.

At 6:30 p.m. of the following day, Heidegger took a cab to the Cooper Union and was met by Brenda Lasch. "How do you do," she said, in a curiously detached, aloof tone. Heidegger noted that she seemed to be wearing too much makeup. She held her head quite high, and he sensed that she regarded him with some contempt. He was led to the stage, on which had been placed two lecterns with a chair next to each. Heidegger was directed to sit in the one on the left. He noticed that there was a long table covered with books off to the side of the hall. "May I get you something to drink?" asked Mrs. Lasch. Heidegger declined her offer, but asked if he could take a look at the books, as there were still some minutes to kill. "Of course," she said and led Heidegger over. A young, bookish man in large glasses sat behind the table, obviously in charge of selling the books. Heidegger got a jolt when his eyes settled on the volume closest to him: *The Eternal Source* by Dagmar Ertl. The cover art looked remarkably like Soviet realism. It depicted a nude man hefting an enormous length of pipe underneath a stylized sun.

Now this rang a bell. Dagmar Ertl had been a big sensation in America some fifteen years earlier. *The Eternal Source*, her first novel, was a bestseller. Elfride had read the German translation and given Heidegger a detailed description of the plot.

The hero of *The Eternal Source* was an engineer named Finn McCool who had won the task of building an oil pipeline through Yosemite National Park. The villain was a zealous ecologist named Measley Swillspittle who tried everything to destroy McCool and his plans. Heidegger remembered Elfride describing the incredibly vivid scenes in which forests and mountains were blasted to dust in order to make way for the pipeline. She had read aloud one portion to him in which the hero and heroine made love on a pile of dynamite, destined the following morning to destroy an Indian burial mound. The love interest was a ballerina named Aryana Frost. Initially, Aryana resists McCool, and even attempts to destroy him through dance. In the end, however, she joins him and together they dynamite a dam, flooding a nearby home for subnormal children. At his trial, McCool makes a heroic speech arguing for "man's right to do as he damn well pleases." McCool is acquitted, and Swillspittel commits suicide by taking an overdose of bromides. In the final, justifiably famous scene, McCool makes violent love to Aryana and, in a gesture symbolic of what Ertl called "man's pioneering spirit," her screams break the sound barrier.

Ertl was born Rosa Sternblatt in Latvia in 1904. In her autobiography, *And I Mean It!* (1959) she had claimed that she left Latvia due to an anti-Semitic pogrom. In fact, subsequent research has revealed that there was no pogrom, and that the inhabitants of Ertl's town meant to kill her alone. In any case, on immigrating to the United States in 1924 she took the name Dagmar Ertl, which she had lifted, along with two hundred and fifty dollars, from a Norwegian woman she bumped into on Ellis Island. From there, it was off to Hollywood, where Ertl worked as stuntwoman in numerous silent films, largely owing to her uncanny resemblance to Fatty Arbuckle. All the while, however, she yearned to be a screenwriter. In 1928, she sold a screen treatment to Paramount, which the studio bought as a possible vehicle for Zazu Pitts. Entitled *I Will Scourge You!* the story centered around the headmistress of a school for the daughters of Sweden's nobility. Ertl later adapted it into a short story, "Whatever You Do Don't Scourge Me!" A brief excerpt from that story, which was not published until after Ertl's death, will give some indication of its flavor:

> After her confession, Greta was taken to the Correction Wing. Anna awaited her, a short leather whip gripped tightly in her left hand. "Do you know why you have been brought here?" she asked the girl.
> "Yes. Because I dared to tie a knot that could not be untied," Greta replied, trembling.
> "You have confessed. But that is only part of what we ask. You must also repent of your crime."
> Greta threw her head back and laughed—and, oh! There never was such laughter. "I do not repent my deeds. In fact, tomorrow I shall build a mountain that I cannot climb over."
> "Remove her garments!" cried Anna to the two sturdy matrons. Greta was

stripped to the waist and chained to the cold, brick wall. When Anna's lash came down on her she felt as if her heart would leave her body. Again and again it came down. And the entire time, the one thought that was at the center of Greta's mind was her secret love for Anna, and her dream that one day, together, they might desalinize the Atlantic.

I Will Scourge You! was never filmed. In 1935, Ertl began writing *The Eternal Source*, which was originally entitled *Blast!* It took Ertl seven years just to complete the first paragraph:

Finn McCool washed. He stood naked in his shower. From some far off place he heard the sound of a man singing. *She'll be comin' round the mountain when she comes, she'll be comin' round the mountain when she comes . . .* Then he realized the singing came from himself. That morning he had lost his license to practice engineering in all forty eight states. This had been the result of a judge's decision in a court case that had dragged on for thirteen months. McCool had been hired to rationalize the system of tunnels that meandered through the San Diego zoo, enabling the keepers to enter and leave cages, feeding and caring for the animals. The zoo's board of directors, a group of grey men in even greyer suits, had ordered McCool not to alter the zoo's basic structure. McCool responded early one Sunday morning. He had hired a fleet of bulldozers from all over San Diego. At precisely six a.m., McCool had blown a whistle and the bulldozers had charged forward, sweeping away the entire zoo: buildings, trees, and animals. The inhabitants of San Diego awoke that morning to find a huge wall of rubble and writhing limbs rushing across town. The noise was said to have been incredible. In the end, McCool had been found by the police standing on top of a pile of zebras. "Arrest me," he said. "I'll talk at the trial."

Initially, when it was finally published in 1944, *The Eternal Source* was coolly received. However, by word of mouth (especially, strange to say, among the inmates of American prisons) sales began to pick up, until one year later the novel had become a bestseller. Ertl was suddenly catapulted to celebrity.

Immediately, she began work on her next novel. In the process of planning it, Ertl realized that she needed to work out her philosophy more fully. Critics had called *The Eternal Source* an expression of "atomic individualism." Gradually, Ertl began to take these words to heart. She developed the philosophy she would later christen *atomic realism*. At a meeting with her publishers, Ertl was asked if she could explain her philosophy while standing on one hand. She is said to have done so as follows:

Metaphysics: All that exists is atoms
    and empty space.
Epistemology: Realism—our senses are
    acted upon by the atoms.
Ethics: Act atomically and return
    things to the atoms.
Politics: Every man for himself.

Unaware that she was reinventing Epicureanism, Ertl declared that everything is made out of atoms. Change is just a rearrangement of the atoms, which are deathless. The processes that bring about change are predictable, but are purely mechanical and without purpose. There is thus no God and also no soul. Man is but a plaything of the atoms, and every aspect of his character is determined by forces beyond his control. There is a strange conflict, however, between these metaphysical theses and the ethical claims of Ertl's philosophy. Ertl does not seem to realize that the assertion that man is completely determined is incompatible with the idea that man is a heroic being. On the one hand, she is a strict determinist, on the other, a moralist who expounds on what men should and should not do. The characters in her novels are all heroic men of action who look down upon the "do-nothings" and "leeches."

The chief commandment of Ertl's ethics is "act atomically," which means that one should strive to be as independent as possible. Ertl's followers, who call themselves "students of atomic realism," sometimes take this to absurd extremes. Many have become hermits, avoiding all human contact. Ertl also enjoins her followers to "return things to the atoms," by which she means to destroy things by breaking them down into their constituents, from which something new and useful might be constructed. She explains this concept in a work from the 1960s, *Introduction to Atomic Realist Metaphysics*:

> As a useful example, take an old chair. It may be broken up and its wood components used to make pencils, matches, or to serve as kindling in a fire. An organization may be broken up. Its members can make up a new, more efficient organization. Or take the body of an old man. His organs may be harvested to save the lives of others, or to be used in medical research. In general, we have an obligation to facilitate the rearrangement of matter. In fact, if man has a cosmic destiny (and I use this phrase only figuratively) it would be this: to be the *nous* of the world, facilitating the soulless processes that

draw the atoms apart and separate them. But note that man must be *nous*, or mind. Mindless destruction cannot be justified.

The trouble was that many of the characters in her novels engaged in acts that looked precisely like mindless destruction. And the "students of atomic realism," predictably, were forever getting in the papers after dynamiting this or that. In a 1961 interview with *Screw* magazine, Ertl was compelled to defend herself against the charge that she encouraged violence in her followers.

Though *The Eternal Source* had gained Ertl notoriety, it is not the novel her followers regard as her masterwork. That honor belongs to the novel she would publish some fourteen years later, in 1958, *Atomic Titan*. Some 3,000 pages long, it was issued by Doubleday in two volumes, with a handsome box to hold them. Paperback copies are usually sold with a small magnifying glass.

Atomic Titan is the story of Titania Baggins, a woman who has inherited a fleet of majestic Zeppelins. While struggling to keep her company airborne in the face of stiff competition from the airline, train, and shipping industries, Titania discovers a mysterious conspiracy to rid the world of the color green. Clothiers have been bought off, and refuse to manufacture green clothes. American money turns red, eyeshades turn blue, and passengers on steamships turn orange. One day, Titania awakens to find her front lawn brown, along with the entire countryside. Her crewmen begin talking about the "Dutchman," a phantom Zeppelin seen only at night, which has been bedeviling air traffic. Having heard such tales before, Titania dismisses them as superstition. But one day, while picnicking in the Scottish Highlands, Titania comes across a strange encampment, around which are strewn barrels marked "BG-30." She hides and waits until nightfall, only to see a black Zeppelin touch down. Secreting herself inside the craft, she discovers that the airship is piloted by a handsome rogue named Lars von der Vogelweide. BG-30 is the chemical he is using to turn green vegetation brown. Titania attacks Lars with a hammer, but he subdues her, and the Zeppelin soon returns them to his lair, which is concealed inside a huge, disused water tower. There, among the barrels of BG-30, Lars makes violent love to Titania. Afterwards, she demands to know his plan. "There is no plan," he confesses. "I took the green . . . because it's there!"

This is a recurring theme in Ertl's work, and critics seize upon it to argue that despite her protestations she does indeed condone senseless destruction. In any case, Titania joins Lars. She enlists her fleet of Zeppelins to spread BG-30 across the entire European continent. After an exciting ski chase

"New York"

in which Lars and Titania are almost apprehended by the Austrian police, the pair escape into Switzerland and amuse themselves by poisoning wells. After mooring the largest Zeppelin in the world to the top of the Eiffel Tower, Lars and Titania rain death down on the inhabitants of Paris in the form of helium balloons carrying fragile wax balls filled with hydrochloric acid. Finally, they are captured just as Titania is about to torpedo a steamship filled with microcephalics. Lars agrees to cooperate with the police and explain to them how to counteract the effects of BG-30, if they will allow him to address the world by radio. There follows what to Ertl's followers is the highpoint of the novel, and to her detractors the low point. Lars von der Vogelweide's speech lasts for four hundred and eleven pages. He expounds the philosophy of atomic realism, but also much else. Ertl includes not only metaphysics, epistemology, ethics, and politics, but also aesthetics, philosophy of mind, philosophy of science, philosophy of history, speculative physics, botany, zoology, origami, and wine making. At one point, Lars pauses to gargle and Ertl inserts a cake recipe. This is followed by a response to anticipated criticisms of the novel, followed by a denunciation of waste in the dairy industry.

A few excerpts will suffice to indicate the tone of Lars's speech. Lars on metaphysics:

Atoms atom and the conceptual articulation of that axiom implies three correlative lemmas: that atoms are, that nothing else is save empty space (viz. nothing), and that human beings exist possessing consciousness characterized by cognitive powers constituted by the atoms, and for the cognition of the atoms, consciousness being the faculty of perceiving aggregates of atoms.

Lars on ethics:

Do I hear you say that you want to be with others? Of all your sins that is the one which damns you most of all. The voice that cries out from the heart "let me love," "let me be with others," "let me not be alone" this is the voice of imbecility and moral decay. Do you hear ringing in your ears the "thou shalt" that commands that you cleave to your brethren? To this I issue a new "thou shalt": thou shalt be as the atoms! Independent, impenetrable, indivisible, approaching others but never touching. Do you call the life that I demand harsh and unforgiving? To this I respond: *and how!*

Lars on the history of philosophy:

The first of the great annihilators was your Anaximander, who declared all things to be a soupy oneness. He was

"New York"

followed by a drooling swami named Heraclitus, whose woozy jottings on the flux abandoned reason altogether. Finally, a new dawn came with Democritus, which was quickly forgotten when men crawled down into the muck of Plato's cave. Plato! That foulest of all foul deceivers, who denied the world and the atoms to make room for a netherworld of fantasies and his God. Western philosophy has mostly followed Plato's example, damning the atoms, damning sense, damning man, damning it all! And this is what you call enlightenment? Sorry kids, but no cigar!

Lars on cuisine:

Take the hamburger sandwich, for instance. In contrast to the decadent soufflé or casserole, in which all sense of distinction is eliminated, the hamburger sandwich is a tower of distinct elements, each of which retains its specific identity and can be recombined to form a new meal. It is no accident that this culinary masterpiece has come to symbolize America all over the world. America! A land where a man can live as he pleases, for what he pleases, fenced off from his neighbor, closed within his abode, not giving a damn about anyone. All you who hear me, all of you have gained in your lives either directly or indirectly from this great nation, all of you should take five minutes and give silent thanks before the fattest, greasiest hamburger sandwich you can find!

The speech concludes with Lars commanding his listeners, "To a gas chamber go!" Afterwards, Ballsak, the President of Earth and Rotating Premier of the Sun System, implores Lars to take over and lead the world. Lars refuses and, in a dramatic scene, he and Titania escape from the General Assembly building of the United World Agency. In an autogiro, they head for Lars's Fortress of Solitude in the arctic. There, Lars has built an enormous generator, powered by sunlight reflected off snow. A huge cable extends from the heart of the generator to the Arctic Ocean, where it disappears beneath the ice caps. His plan is to electrify the world's oceans and kill every last living thing in them, again because "it's there." Titania, however, decides that this time he has gone too far. At first she tries to dissuade him, but is unsuccessful. Just as he is about to throw the switch, she launches herself at him with a crowbar. As they scuffle, Titania accidentally falls on the switch, turning on the generator and electrifying the oceans. On closed circuit television they watch as billions of fish and other sea creatures fly up and out of the world's oceans in their death throes. Titania achieves sexual climax for the first time, and, in the novel's final scene, falls to her knees and makes an oath of fealty to Lars.

To put it mildly, the reviews of *Atomic Titan* were brutal. It was denounced from the pages of every newspaper in America, and abroad. "Nietzsche meets the Marquis de Sade," opined the *New York Times*. Ertl's relatives in Latvia received permission to visit America so that they could argue in court for having her committed. The case was thrown out. Then the great "Ertl death threat" craze of the fall of '58 began. It started with some anonymous notes mailed to her publisher, Mortimer Snerd. "ERTEL [sic] I WILL KILL YOU YOU ARE MONSTER," one read. The message was formed out of letters cut from a magazine. This was reported in the media nationwide. Radio commentator Walter Winchell did a story on the death threats, ending with the comment, "For my money, it would be poetic justice if somebody knocked off this colossal misanthrope. Gee whiz, I might even do it myself!" This was followed three days later by a similar editorial comment by Edward R. Murrow, who also ended by threatening to kill Ertl. Within a week, other journalists and even Hollywood stars were openly expressing their desire to kill the author. "I'd stab her in the heart if she had one," quipped Steve Allen. "Yes, I'd like to kill her. No I haven't read the novel," said Jayne Mansfield in response to a reporter who stopped her at a premiere. "Kill her!" shouted a grinning Vice President Nixon as he boarded a helicopter on the White House lawn.

For the rest of 1958 and into 1959, Ertl had to hire bodyguards to protect her everywhere she went. One of these bodyguards was a young student working his way through New York University. His name was Avi Fischbein. A psychology major, he had come across Ertl's work when one of his professors had said, "Oh, you must read her. She's insane." He had devoured *The Eternal Source* in a single day. That was in 1957. When *Atomic Titan* was published, he bought a copy on the very first day it was offered for sale, just as the bookstore opened. While working as Ertl's bodyguard he tried several times to engage her in conversation, but each time she rebuffed him by hitting him in the face with a pie. So he tried an indirect route by getting to know Ertl's husband, Lamus.

Ertl married Lamus O'Geldinng in 1928. Once described as the least funny vaudevillian of them all, he had given up the stage many years earlier and was now an embittered morphine addict. He would shoot up openly, in front of Ertl and her friends and bodyguards. "Lamus needs another vitamin shot!" she would say, and scratch his chin with her long fingernails. Avi confided in Lamus that he desperately wanted to get to know Ertl. "Then fuck her," Lamus replied.

"New York"

Avi was a handsome, brown-haired, brown-eyed Jewish boy of twenty-one. By contrast, Dagmar Ertl was fifty-five years old. She weighed three hundred pounds and stank of herring. Her hair was long and stringy and unkempt, her clothes tattered and covered with grave mould. Nevertheless, a mutual attraction developed. Ertl discovered that this boy understood her ideas better than her own husband, or any man she had ever met. Soon, they began an affair, though this was unknown to Heidegger and to most of the world. There was only one complication: Avi's young wife Brenda. He solved this problem easily enough by drugging the warm milk she drank each night before going to bed, and racing across town to be with Ertl.

By the spring of 1961, at Ertl's suggestion, Avi had changed his name to Rensselaer Lasch and had established the Rensselaer Lasch Institute, which distributed lectures on Ertl's philosophy. A circle of admirers formed around Ertl. Known as "the atom smashers," they met regularly for discussions in Ertl's apartment. Each meeting followed the same pattern. The members of the group would roll up their sleeves to reveal Ertl's personal symbol, which had been branded on each of them:

Ertl herself wore the symbol, in the form of a gold brooch. The "atom smashers" would then trample on a cross and say the Lord's Prayer backwards. The evening would climax with each of them coming forward to kiss Ertl's rump. Afterwards, they would snack on mounds of sweet pastries, drink expresso, smoke a great deal, and then go home around dawn. Every so often a member would be suspected of some form of deviationism, whereupon a "trial" would be held in Ertl's apartment, presided over by Lasch. The guilty party would then be baked by Ertl in a pie. At least, such were the rumors . . .

"Professor Heidegger?" said a stiff, male voice.

Heidegger was startled. He turned around to see a largish man staring at him. He had a head that seemed too big for his body, a shock of silver hair, and penetrating eyes. "I am Rensselaer Lasch." He did not smile on introducing himself, or even extend his hand. He gave Heidegger every impression that he found dealing with him a distasteful duty. "Would you care to approach your lectern? We are about to begin." Heidegger did as he was asked. By this point, the hall had almost filled to capacity, and the attendees were busily chatting amongst themselves. Suddenly, a hush fell over the room. Dagmar Ertl had entered, accompanied by several of the "atom smashers." She wore a black cloak emblazoned with the "atomic" pin, what looked like a Napoleonic tricorn hat, and wooden shoes. Three wolfhounds nipped at her heels. She and her entourage sat down in the front row, then Ertl nodded and smiled at Lasch.

Lasch cleared his throat and began. After thanking the organizers, he announced the topic of the debate. "We are here tonight to debate a question that is of the utmost importance to human life on this earth. Our topic is: Being or beings. Being or beings. That is our question. My opponent, Martin Heidegger," here his voice rose as if he were a prosecutor denouncing the foulest of criminals, "has denied that beings exist and believes only in a mystical Being which, he says, is nothing!"

Heidegger frowned at this.

Lasch immediately held up a copy of "What is Metaphysics?" "Do you deny it?! It's all here in black and white, sir! Professor Heidegger has denied the undeniable: he has denied the existence of the primal, atomic beings, and proclaimed the void as the only reality!"

After Lasch had finished his tirade, Heidegger patiently explained that he had not denied that beings exist, he had merely drawn a distinction between beings and Being. He also explained that he had indeed said that Being is nothing but only because it is not a being, and hence no-thing. This was accompanied by much eye-rolling and sighing by Lasch, as well as hisses from the audience. Every time Lasch finished a point, the audience would applaud tumultuously. All Heidegger could do was to calmly respond to each of the confusions and distortions present in Lasch's utterances. An hour into the debate he felt dizzy.

Afterwards, a crowd of admirers gathered around Lasch, but Ertl left quickly, protected by her entourage. Heidegger noticed that as she turned to leave, she blew a quick kiss to Lasch with her gloved hand, then grabbed her crotch and gave a wolf whistle. Heidegger thought this odd, but gave it no further thought. He was left standing alone at his lectern. After a few minutes, Lasch approached him looking like the proverbial cat that had swallowed the canary. He slapped Heidegger on the arm. "Well, Professor. Miss Ertl has asked me to invite you back to her apartment for a little celebration. We atomic realists can be gracious in victory." Heidegger was about to decline, but then he thought that it might be interesting, and accepted.

An hour later Heidegger's cab deposited

him at an apartment house on East Thirty-fourth Street. The doorman announced him, and soon he was being ushered into Dagmar Ertl's seventh floor apartment. The living room was smaller than he expected, and filled with starkly modern furniture. Electric blue polka dots, Ertl's favorite design, dominated the room. A cloud of cigarette smoke hung in the air. "Greetings, Professor Heidegger!" Ertl herself was now approaching him, a hand held out to shake his. Her eyes were not as penetrating as they had been described to him. In fact, they looked rather filmy or oily to him, as if the orbs were swimming in mucous. She spoke to him in English, though Heidegger had heard that she was fluent in German, and also spoke a passable Mandarin. "Vould you like a lady finger?" she said, in her thick Latvian accent. A black woman dressed in a frilly French maid's outfit offered him a plate, which he declined. Ertl chatted with him pleasantly about his trip to the United States, and about the brief time she had spent in Germany after leaving Latvia. Heidegger had the impression that she was deliberately avoiding intellectual matters because she did not regard him as a worthy interlocutor. She kept patting his arm and speaking to him very gently, as if he had been wounded or were convalescing.

After a few minutes, she left him and went to mingle with the other guests. Heidegger discovered that if he pressed his nose to the window he could just see the tip of the nose of the person pressed to the window of the apartment in the building opposite. He wanted to avoid looking at the guests. The entire affair had the feeling of a wake rather than a party. All that was missing was the coffin in the center of the room.

"Are you enjoying yourself?" Brenda Lasch had approached him from behind. Heidegger turned to look at her. Her head was held so high he thought it remarkable that her nose wasn't bleeding. "Let me introduce you to the Chairman of the Federal Reserve," she said, taking Heidegger's arm.

Suddenly, Dagmar Ertl climbed on top of a chair and called out to the room. "Listen, everyone! I'm sorry to interrupt your gay merry making, but I hef an important announcement. Please be seated." The entire room obeyed her at once. Lamus O'Geldinng appeared, festooned with crumbs, and produced a small stool for Heidegger to sit on. "I hef been vaiting for ze proper moment to tell you all zis, and I suppose tonight vill hef to do," Ertl continued. "A veek ago I vas playing Tiddly Vinks vith Lamus and suddenly I fell over ze board and vent into a trance."

At this the room gasped.

"I lost consciousness briefly, but then found myself floating down a long tunnel. Zer vas a bright light at the end of it, and pretty music vas playing—music I hef not heard since I vas a girl in Latvia. As I got furzer down ze tunnel, a figure appeared at ze end. Ven I got closer I recognized him. Who do you suppose it vas? It vas Jesus! He vas vearing dark blue coveralls and he carried a T-square. As I approached, he took me by the hand and said to me, 'You hef been a very naughty girl, Rosa.' Zat's my real name, you see. 'You must be punished.'

"Instantly I vas sent off to Purgatory. I vas stripped of my garments, stuffed into a kind of pod, and then lashed repeatedly by shirtless musclemen in black leather masks. After zat I vas forced to get down on my hands and scrub all of heaven. 'Scrub it clean, bitch,' said Jesus. 'Now scrub my boot,' he said, sticking it out in front of me. 'No lick, it.' Vell, I vill spare you all ze details. Anyvay, he told me zat it vas not yet my time, and that zis vas but a foretaste. After zat, he took my hand and ve flew out over ze clouds, over ze whole earth. Zen ve flew under ze earth and into Hell. 'Zis is where naughty girls go,' Jesus said to me.

"Hell vas a horrible place! It vas filled vith writhing, naked bodies undergoing unimaginable torments. It smelled worse zan anything you could imagine. Zer ver seven million dungeons in hell, vith seven hundred thousand chambers in each dungeon, and seventy thousand cells visin each chamber, and each chamber had seven thousand forms of torture and every poor soul suffered seven hundred stabbing pains every seven milliseconds. I'm telling you, it vas bad!

"Zen ve vent to see ze devil himself. He

vas several miles tall, so zat ven ve stood at his feet, ve couldn't see his head. Jesus miracled me up to ze devil's ass, and I spent awhile hovering around ze outside of it. Just as I was becoming veak vith fear, ze devil broke vind.

Ze blast blew me out of hell, and as I sailed across ze world at incredible speed, I heard Jesus call to me, and he said: 'Be a good girl now, Rosa. Renounce your atheist philosophy and dedicate yourself to good vorks. Renounce your lover Lasch and return to your faithful husband Lamus. You and Lamus must go around ze vorld proclaiming ze Good News from out of a tent for ze rest of your life. Zat is ze only vay you can get through ze pearly gates.'

"Zen I avoke vith my head on ze Tiddly Vinks board and found Lamus giving himself a vitamin shot." As she said these final sentences, she removed the gold "atomic" brooch from her cape, and pinned a crucifix in its place.

Heidegger looked around the room. There was dead silence. No one spoke. He looked to his left and noticed that Rensselaer Lasch lay unconscious on the carpet by the credenza.

Dagmar Ertl was now dancing around in a circle and clapping her hands, singing:

♪ People get ready . . . Jesus is comin'!
Soon we'll be goin' home.
People get ready . . .

"New York"

Jesus is comin'!
To take from the world His own.

People get ready . . . Jesus is comin'!
Soon we'll be goin' home . . . ♪

Heidegger in Chicago

"I asked you once, during Germany's darkest hour, to join me. You refused."

CHAPTER SIX

"Chicago"

The day after the debacle at the Cooper Union, Heidegger made his notorious appearance on *What's My Line?* Once the episode was taped, Heidegger made plans to rendezvous for dinner with Dorothy Kilgallen and Bennet Cerf. He was glad that Arlene Francis had bowed out, since she had mistaken him for Jean-Paul Sartre. John Daly's assistant, Coco Goya, was to serve as his guide.

It was late in the afternoon when she hailed a cab for the two of them. Coco said nothing to Heidegger during the entire trip. He was somewhat puzzled when the cab pulled up in front of a tattoo parlor on St. Mark's Place, next door to an Afghan restaurant. Coco paid the driver and they got out. "This way," she said, and led Heidegger down a short flight of steps into the tattoo parlor.

It was empty, except for the employees, most of whom were male. Their heads had been buzzcut until the skin showed, and all of them wore black tee shirts. The room was lined with mirrors and small squares pinned to the walls, depicting various designs which, for a price, one could choose to have permanently etched into one's skin. Moving quickly, Coco led Heidegger through a curtain at the back of the shop. She stopped before a mirror in an alcove which reached from floor to ceiling. On each side of the alcove were light switches. Coco reached out both of her arms and simultaneously flipped the switches up. Without making a sound, the mirror slid up into the ceiling, revealing a long corridor lined with what appeared to be steel.

Coco beckoned for Heidegger to enter the corridor. The mirror HISSED down into the floor behind them, and they moved forward. The steel wall at the opposite end now slid aside, and a ginger colored cat darted out and into their path. As they approached the open passage, Heidegger heard the sound of what must have been several dozen cats mewing and purring inside the room beyond. From her bag, Coco removed a small Beretta and pointed it straight at Heidegger's heart. "I'm sorry to have to do this, Professor. Step inside, and don't try anything heroic."

The room was bathed in a soft, blue light. It was empty, except for one curious item. Dominating the middle of the room was what appeared to be a large, black, featureless globe set into a round stand. The globe began to swivel around, and Heidegger real-

"Chicago"

ized that it was open on one side and that the globe was actually a chair. Seated in it was a small, elderly, birdlike woman wearing an Indian sari and earrings which, on closer inspection, proved to be swastikas. Two cats were lounging on the dark cushion in the chair, on either side of the woman. At least thirty others were winding their way around the chair and throughout the room. The mysterious woman pressed a hidden switch and the steel door slid shut.

She smiled at Heidegger. "I will not tell you my name, Professor Heidegger. But they call me . . . the Cat Lady."

The hair stood up on Heidegger's back. He had heard this alias before. When was it? Yes, just after the war. In connection with Operation Werewolf, the short-lived Nazi resistance movement that had carried out acts of sabotage against the Allied occupiers. The ring leader of the group near Freiburg was supposed to have been code named "Die Katzefrau." Once, on a night in 1945, when the moon had been full, a black Mercedes had pulled up at the bottom of the hill, below Heidegger's Todtnauberg hut. The driver had released a cat, and then driven away. Heidegger had found it playing near the well. Attached to its collar was a message:

> Join us, Professor Heidegger, in our fight against the Allied hordes. Become our spiritual leader. If you wish to do so, go to the town square and shout

three times "I wish to join Operation Werewolf" at mid-day tomorrow. Remember, he who is not with us is against us.

(signed) The Cat Lady

Heidegger considered this manner of communicating with Werewolf a trifle too risky. And, besides, he knew that Germany had lost and that continuing to fight would only make the lot of the ordinary German even worse. He had heard nothing else from the Cat Lady, until today.
"I see by the look on your face that you remember me," she said. "Good. I asked you once, during Germany's darkest hour, to join me. You declined. I have chosen to overlook this. But now you are even more famous and celebrated than you were then. I have summoned you here to ask you to join our cause. Not the cause of Germany but of the entire Aryan race, as it faces what could well be its Ragnarok. Did you get the Viewmasters I sent you from the Cotswalds? No matter."
Heidegger turned and glared at Coco Goya, who lowered her eyes. "I'm sorry, Professor Heidegger," she said, choking back tears. "But she has my father, Dr. Cosmo Goya, the inventor of the Helio Beam. Werewolf has been trying to break him for months."
The Cat Lady leaned back in her chair

and crossed her legs. "It's a pity. I wanted that Helio Beam in orbit by Labor Day. Unfortunately, it looks like we'll have to wait. Dr. Goya is being very uncooperative. So far, I've refrained from using . . . extreme measures."

Coco moved closer to Heidegger. "She promised they might release him if I cooperated and brought you here." Heidegger looked at her as if to say, "You little fool . . ."

The Cat Lady now rose from the chair, sending several felines scurrying away. "Now I must put my proposal to you again. This time with a twist: Join us . . . or die."

Heidegger crossed his arms and looked away. Slowly, patiently, he explained why it had been a mistake for him to ever have involved himself in a political cause, and why he would never do so again. He added that he had vowed never to speak on this subject, and seemed quite angry that the Cat Lady had forced him into doing so.

She laughed after hearing his speech. "If you want it that way, so be it." She clapped her hands. The steel door slid aside and three of the men they had seen in the tattoo parlor came sauntering in, their arms crossed over their barrel chests. "Skinheads, subdue them!" cried the Cat Lady.

Coco winked at Heidegger and lashed out with a powerful karate kick at the skinhead nearest her. He crumpled to the floor. Heidegger grabbed a notebook and hurled it like a boomerang at another of the louts, hitting him in the right eye.

"Stop! *Kallifee!*" cried the Cat Lady, using an obscure Indian dialect. "Seize them you fools, they're getting away . . . !" But Heidegger and Coco were already gone, slipping out through a flimsy, unlocked screen door at the back of the Cat Lady's impregnable stainless steel lair.

Needless to say, Heidegger missed his dinner with Bennett Cerf and Dorothy Kilgallen. He considered himself lucky to have escaped the clutches of the Cat Lady and decided it was imperative that he put some distance between himself and New York at once. So, with no idea what else to do, he took a cab to LaGuardia Airport and booked the next flight to Chicago, the final stop on his American tour. He had no idea what would happen when he arrived there—no idea if the Cat Lady and Werewolf would be waiting.

He needed help. The trouble was that Heidegger had no one in America he felt he could trust to advise him about where to go, whom to associate with, and whom to avoid. At least that was until he met Charles Manson.

Manson had been paroled six months earlier, pardoned in a final act of malice by an unpopular governor voted ignominiously out of office. Greeted on the outside by a few of his old followers, he had been whisked away from reporters in a brand new, black Mercedes bus. After three months, however, he had parted company with them. "Man, I was gettin' tired of those people back in 1969," he told Larry King on national television. Asked what his plans were, he had said that he intended to spend his time saving air, trees, water, and animals. Unfortunately, this did not translate into gainful employment, and he wound up working at a Starbucks counter at the Los Angeles International Airport.

By an odd quirk that could happen only in American aviation, Heidegger's travel itinerary from New York's LaGuardia to O'Hare Airport in Chicago required him to fly first to LAX and wait three hours before taking a connecting flight to his final destination. He had brought a signed copy of *Atomic Titan* to read on the plane, but tired of it once he reached Lars's speech.

When his plane touched down at LAX, Heidegger went straight to a newsstand to find some different reading material. While standing there, glancing through a new Danielle Steel offering, he overheard an altercation across the terminal walkway. A woman seemed to be involved in an argument with a scraggly haired man working behind the Starbuck's counter.

"I told you I want a grande, skinny, decaf latte with a shot of amaretto," the woman said sharply, her hands on her hips.

"Now why do you want that?" the man responded, almost tenderly.

"Just give me the drink, please."

"I am that drink! I am grande. I am amaretto. And you are too, and we are one, you dig?" the short, scraggly man replied.

At this point the manager—a tall black man with an exaggeratedly dignified manner—came over and asked what the problem was. He put a hand on the employee's shoulder, but the man recoiled violently.

"You don't wanna touch me, brotha, 'cause I'm as cold as ice and as sharp as a razor on a moonlit night!" Then the man began to gyrate oddly, bobbing and weaving and generally acting deranged.

"That's it, Manson. You're fired!" the manager declared.

Manson ripped his apron off and went stalking out from behind the counter and down the walkway. When he came to the newsstand, he stopped suddenly. "You're Martin Heidegger, aren't you?

Heidegger turned and replied that yes, indeed, he was.

"Man, I've been readin' you for years. Just years! I've spent most of my life in prison, which gives you a lot of time to read. I've been through everything by you that's been translated. My favorite is *Introduction to Metaphysics*. I must've read that twelve or fifteen times in the clink. I know it by heart. My favorite line is 'The works that are being peddled about nowadays as the philosophy of National Socialism but have nothing to do with the inner truth and greatness of this movement (namely the encounter between global technology and modern man)—have all been written by men fishing in the troubled waters of 'values' and 'totalities.'" At this, Heidegger blushed. Then he noticed, for the first time, the swastika carved into the man's forehead. He considered running off, but something about the man appealed to him. They found a quiet place to sit down and began chatting. Heidegger was surprised when he glanced at his watch and realized that an hour had gone by.

"I know what you mean, pal. I know exactly what you're talking about," Manson said, touching Heidegger's arm. "This country is fucked up. You shouldn't a been flyin' all over this way and that, speakin' where anybody said, jumpin' when they said jump. You shoulda had an agent." Heidegger frowned at this. "You know, a manager. A guy who's got connections and who can make deals for you." Heidegger asked Manson if he had connections. "Sure I do! Everybody in the country knows who I am."

Heidegger said that he wished he had met Manson earlier, but that he was winding up his American tour with the Chicago visit.

"You ever been to Chicago?" Manson asked, leaning in close. Heidegger had to admit that he hadn't. "It's a jungle, man. A jungle. One of the most dangerous places in America. And this time do you know anything about the outfit that's invited you?" Heidegger told him that it was the University

Heidegger in Chicago

"Man, I've been reading you for years.
I've spent more of my life in prison, which
gives you a lot of time to read."

"Chicago"

of Chicago, but that he had never heard of most of the professors who were playing host to him. "See there? That's just what I'm talking about. You have no idea what you're getting into. I have a proposal. Take me along to Chicago with you and I'll act as your guide, your manager, and your bodyguard, all in one. All I ask for in exchange is that you pay my expenses. I'm going to need plane fare, a hotel room, 420, and a shitload of Mars bars."

Heidegger fell silent for a while, considering Manson's proposal. Although he had only one more American city to visit before, blessedly, returning to Germany, his nerves were so jangled after what had happened in New York he felt he could use a companion to take care of details for him. Manson seemed like a reliable sort, and the man had a profound understanding of his philosophy. A few minutes earlier, he had jotted down an expression Manson had used, referring to language as "the house of being."

Heidegger was pleasantly surprised to find that there were still seats available on the flight to Chicago, and he purchased the empty seat next to him for Manson. Then he bought the Danielle Steel novel.

On the plane, Manson said little to Heidegger. Instead, he spent his time scribbling in a notebook. Heidegger asked him what he was doing. "I'm makin' a list of all the people we should call when we get to Chicago." He handed it to Heidegger. At the top of the list was J. Edgar Hoover. "I want Hoover over for tea. Like tea with the Queen. Crumpets and everything." Deciding to humor him, Heidegger said that he doubted Mr. Hoover would be willing to join them. "Of course he will! You're a famous philosopher. You're the bait. I'm the hook." The next name on Manson's list was Bing Crosby. "He'll serenade us as we sip daiquiris on the hotel balcony." Heidegger had to smile at the man's childlike notions. "Here, look. I've drawn a security diagram of the hotel." To Heidegger, it looked like a sketch of the inside of a television set. "And we have to decide on the route your motorcade will take. For instance, do we drive by the book depository, or not by the book depository?" He was silent for a while. "You know Oswald?" Heidegger said that he did not, but that someone had once tried to show him the Zapruder film. "I knew Oswald. In fact, I was Oswald. I shot JFK, except he wasn't JFK. He was Khrushchev. We're all Khrushchev. We're all that shoe goin' bang bang bang. One really big shoe, that's what life is. Old Ed had it right."

After a few minutes, Heidegger drifted off to sleep.

They landed at O'Hare an hour late. By the time Heidegger had gotten his suitcases and coaxed Manson off the baggage carousel, it was close to midnight. They went outside and Heidegger hailed a taxi. "Why do that?" Manson interjected, leaping in front of him. "It's a beautiful night. Let's walk." But Heidegger insisted on the taxi. He passed the half hour ride to the hotel listening to Manson's account of how the Francis Gary Powers U-2 spy incident had actually been arranged by Motown.

When Heidegger finally opened the door to his hotel room, he found J. Edgar Hoover waiting for him. "I called ahead while you was asleep," Manson explained.

Hoover's face was grim. He rose from the chair by the radiator and greeted Heidegger perfunctorily. "Professor, I must warn you that you may be in danger. Apparently your talks around this country have stirred up a lot of attention. Naturally, I have been monitoring your activities and those of the people who have attended your talks. It appears that somehow you've made a lot of people mad."

Heidegger sat down on the edge of the bed and asked him to explain.

"Well, first of all there's this movie star you toyed with and then abandoned like so much dirty linen. Chinchilla Heatherton? Then there's that couple that kidnapped you. They're still on the loose. Michael Jackson and his staff. The singer Milo Artanis. I have a file on him as thick as his big wop head. There's the faculty of . . . um . . . B.U.L.L.S.H.I.T. There's Hannah Arendt's husband, who claims you're still carrying a torch for her. Uh . . . let me see . . . There's the Cat Lady. Yes, we've been moni-

Heidegger in Chicago

toring her activities for many years now. Oh, and the Duke of Windsor is after you too. Claims you took liberties with his wife. In any case, we have reason to believe that one or more of them may be headed here . . . to kill you."

"What's your evidence, G-man?" cried Manson, dancing forward and dodging left and right.

"The evidence is this . . ." he indicated a four hundred pound gorilla standing in the corner of the room. Until then Heidegger had not noticed it. The gorilla was curiously subdued. "He's been hit with a powerful narcotic. He's still standing, so the lab boys think it's hypnotic rather than soporific. In any case, take a look at what he's holding." In his massive, furry paws the gorilla held a tobacco humidor. Hoover walked over and took the humidor from the ape and passed it to Heidegger. "Open it and sniff." Heidegger did so. There was nothing inside except a few bits of tobacco clinging to the bottom.

"Recognize it?" Hoover asked. Heidegger indicated that he did not. Hoover rolled his eyes. "For a philosophy professor you sure don't know your pipe tobacco. It's Isle of Dogs No. 22. During the Second World War the Allies developed a plan to kill all the professors in Germany as a first step in dumbing down the post-war generation. It was never acted upon, of course, or scum like you wouldn't be killing trees to print your commie bilge. But the radio code phrase that would have put the plan into operation was 'Isle of Dogs.' Someone wants you dead, and they want to make it really obvious."

"What's your advice then?" Manson interjected.

Hoover looked straight at Heidegger. "My advice is for you to cancel your speech here and go back to Germany immediately." He moved forward and pointed a finger at Heidegger's chest. "In fact, if your presence here stirs up any more trouble, I'll have you deported as an undesirable alien. Keep that in mind." He scooped his fedora off the dresser and went to the door, whistling for the gorilla to follow him, which the beast did. "It's been a pleasure, Professor," he said with a wry grin and shut the door behind him.

"Well, can you beat that?" Manson said and climbed up on the radiator.

Now Heidegger was worried. But he would not cancel a public appearance because of vague threats. If it really was true that someone was out to kill him, Heidegger believed it had to be the Cat Lady. Who else would know about the wartime code phrase "Isle of Dogs"?

Realizing that he now had a splitting headache, Heidegger grabbed his medicine bag and headed for the bathroom, the door to which was shut. When he opened it, he was hit by a locomotive. At least that was what the impact felt like. Heidegger was thrown into the room and landed on his back on the carpet. From out of the bathroom leaped a man dressed entirely in black ninja garb, complete with a mask of metal mesh concealing his face. The man wielded a large samurai sword. "HAAAAA!!!" he screamed and leaped toward Heidegger. But the philosopher rolled aside and quickly got to his feet. He grabbed for the telephone on the nightstand and slammed it into the attacker's gut. This doubled the man over, but only for a moment. He took something off his belt and tossed it to the floor, where it erupted in a cloud of white smoke. The man hopped up and over the bed, landing near Manson, who watched the fight with fascination, but made no attempt to help. Heidegger launched himself at the attacker, but wound up crashing into and breaking the glass on the cheap painting over the bed. He landed on the nightstand, demolishing it. The attacker lunged at him with the sword, but Heidegger brought a pillow up to shield himself. It was promptly cut in two, feathers flying everywhere. "Use this!" Manson cried out, throwing Heidegger a copy of the Gideon Bible. Heidegger looked at the book for several seconds, giving his attacker time to leap behind him and wrap a garrote around the philosopher's neck. Heidegger slammed the man in the ribs with his elbow, grabbed his neck with both hands, and tossed him over his shoulder. As the attacker sprawled onto the carpet, his mask fell away.

"Chicago"

"Yukio Mishima!" Manson cried, recognizing Heidegger's attacker as the noted Japanese author.

"Yes, it is I," Mishima said. "I must congratulate you, Heidegger-sensei. You are still in fine form." Years ago, Heidegger had instructed Mishima to attack him unexpectedly, whenever they happened to be in the same city. Together, they had demolished hotel suites in Rome, Stockholm, and Zagreb. But Mishima's attack tonight could not have come at a worse time. Heidegger explained the situation to him.

"Then you must cancel your appearance at the University of Chicago and spend a day with me in the city. I have been given the use of a penthouse suite nearby." Heidegger replied that he was hesitant to cancel any engagement he had already agreed to, but he said that he would consider it. "At least relocate to my penthouse," Mishima said imploringly. Heidegger looked at Manson, and Manson nodded his consent.

The following day, after leaving Mishima's exquisitely tasteful apartment, the trio climbed into the Japanse author's limo to be driven to the University of Chicago. The invitation had come from Leo Strauss, one of Heidegger's former students. At any other time, he would have looked forward to meeting Strauss, but now his heart was filled with angst. Somehow he knew that this day would go badly—very badly. "It is only a short drive," Mishima said.

"How do you know?" Manson barked suspiciously.

Mishima hesitated. "I have occasionally used the sauna in the men's locker room at the university gym. There's ample parking."

"Trouble!" cried Brophy, Mishima's driver and sidekick. Heidegger stared out the window beside him. Several small, identical red convertibles had pulled up alongside them. Heidegger looked across at the other window. The red cars were on the other side as well. In fact, they were in front and in back! The limo was entirely surrounded. Heidegger noticed that the drivers were all wearing rubber pig masks (a reference, he thought to Plato's "city of pigs").

"Henchmen!" cried Manson. Yes, but whose henchmen?

"If only we were in Tokyo and this were my own car, Heidegger-sensei," Mishima cried with despair. "It is bulletproof and fitted out with gun bays and a battering ram."

"I wish I had my dune buggy!" Manson cried.

Mishima leaned forward and gave orders to the driver. "Evasive maneuvers!"

The driver attempted to swerve left and change lanes, trying to force the red cars over. But they didn't budge. The limo slammed into one on the left. It took the impact, swerved away slightly, then came right back. There was no way out.

"Gentleman," Mishima began in a calm tone. "I propose we play along with them, whoever they are. When we get to their destination and the cars are stopped, we can fight our way out. Or at least we can try. It is a good day to die, yes?"

Heidegger and Manson did not answer him. After awhile, Manson spoke quietly without looking at either of them. "Man, I just got outta prison. I don't even think I'm supposed to have left California."

"They're taking us off the freeway," Brophy said. Sure enough, the red cars were taking an exit, forcing the limo along with them. They drove for another half hour, down long country roads that took them far away from any sign of Chicago. At length, they came to a crossroads, and stopped. There was nothing to be seen in any direction, other than acre after acre of corn. Far overhead and to the east, a crop duster, an old-fashioned biplane, was circling back and dusting some farmer's field. The pig men, all of whom were carrying automatic pistols, got out of their cars and ordered the occupants of the limo to get out as well. When Heidegger did so, he noticed that some of the gunmen were women, though all of their faces were still concealed by the masks.

"Over there!" one of them barked, waving his gun barrel in the direction of a cornfield. They all began tromping through the corn. At a certain point, Heidegger looked behind him. They were now so far out into the field that they could never be seen from the road. He wondered if they were all about to executed, gangland style. Suddenly, a horrifying thought occurred to him. Could these masked men be from the A.P.A.? "Face the front, you!" one of them cried. Heidegger did as he was told.

At length, they came to a large patch of ground where it looked like the corn had been mashed down to form a perfect circle. It was the sort of formation that could only be appreciated from the air. Heidegger wondered what could have caused it.

"I caused it!" said the voice of a woman, apparently reading Heidegger's thoughts. One of the henchwomen ripped off her mask to reveal the Cat Lady! Heidegger now realized he should have recognized her from her sari. "I did it with my Zündelsaucer," she said. Heidegger must have looked perplexed, for she continued. "Yes, I can understand your consternation. But you would have learned all about such things had you joined me. The Zündelsaucers, our base in the Antarctic, and, most of all, about the disembodied head of the great man who still leads us."

Heidegger noticed that an empty wooden crate was sitting in the middle of the circle, bottom up. "Go and stand on that. The trial can begin immediately," the Cat Lady said. Hesitantly, Heidegger did as she commanded. Now she pointed her gun at Mishima and Manson. "No heroics from you two." Several of the henchmen were busily searching them for hidden weapons. The Cat Lady

"Chicago"

stepped forward and addressed the group. "Ladies and gentlemen . . . reveal!"

Now all the henchmen and henchwomen removed their masks. Heidegger gasped involuntarily. Present in the circle were Chinchilla Heatherton, Moogoo Hassenpfeffer, Tyler Hassenpfeffer, Michael Jackson, Bertha Kittridge, Peter Badgerhead, Quentin R. DeNameland, Milo Artanis, Furness Meeks, the Duke of Windsor and his equerry, Coco Goya, several skinheads, Rensselaer Lasch, Dagmar Ertl, Lamus O'Geldinng, and a number of others. All of them stared at Heidegger with undisguised malice.

The Cat Lady stood before him. "The crime you have been charged with . . ." She suddenly looked confused and stared at the others. "Exactly what crime do we charge him with?"

"He's not what he seems!" cried a quavering voice. It was Peter Badgerhead.

"I thought he was French! I thought he was . . . sensitive!" wept Chinchilla Heatherton.

Michael Jackson stepped forward. He was wearing his Sergeant Pepper costume. "I thought he was . . . well, on the advice of my attorneys I can't say what I thought he was. But he wasn't that!"

"I thought he was hip," said Milo Artanis, flipping a coin.

"I thought he was committed to social justice," oozed Furness Meeks.

"I thought he was . . . . WROOOONG!"

snarled Rensselaer Lasch.

Each one came forward to complain that Heidegger had not lived up to their expectations, that he had failed them in some way. Each one explained that, much to their disappointment, he was not what they had thought he was.

"And as for myself," said the Cat Lady, slowly approaching Heidegger. "You know what I thought you were. You know what I wanted you to be. Only a god can save us now, you say? Well, it may amuse you to know that today you will be offered to a god. You will be offered to Dionysus! To the god of the corn! To Shiva! To nature herself! To Persephone! We will tear you limb from limb and spread your bloody pieces over this dry earth. You complain of the flight of the gods? Your sacrifice may return them."

Then she fell silent, as did all the others. The Cat Lady moved back to join them. Mishima and Manson stood to one side, unsure of how to act. After what seemed an interminable silence, the Cat Lady cried out in a bloodchilling tone: "KILL HIM!"

All at once, with a kind of animal roar, the crowd rushed for Heidegger. "Oh, what the heck!" Manson cried and joined them. They pulled Heidegger off the box. Chinchilla Heatherton ripped off his left lapel. Bertha Kittridge clutched at his eyes. Dagmar Ertl licked her chops. They pulled his jacket off of him. Hands lifted his feet into the air. . . .

"Chicago"

"Let me be!"

The cry had come from Heidegger. Everyone fell silent and stopped grabbing at him. Hands released him and he fell gently to the earth.

"Let me be!" he cried again. Slowly, he got to his feet, made an effort to compose himself, and stared at them. The crowd began backing away. A cloud passed in the sky overhead and bright sunlight flooded the clearing. Suddenly, everyone present seemed to see Heidegger anew. He was not a rebel, or a hero, or a guru. He was not a twelve year old boy, or a "sensation," or a lyricist, or a sexual acrobat. Neither was he a homosexual, a revolutionary, a Nazi, a liberal, or a nihilist. He was just . . . Heidegger.

Several minutes of silence followed. All that could be heard was the corn moving in the gentle breeze. Then Peter Badgerhead stepped forward, his cap clutched in his fingers. Looking down at the ground, he said, "Professor . . . I think I understand now. And I think I have the words to express it, if you'll forgive my ignorance in advance." Then, in a low, warbling tone he began to sing:

♪ When I find myself in times of trouble
Mother Mary comes to me,
Speaking words of wisdom, let it be. . . .
♪

Now Jackson stepped forward. "Yes," he said quietly. "That's perfect." And he began to sing along:

♪ And when the broken hearted people
Living in the world agree,
There will be an answer, let it be. . . . ♪

Then everyone began to sing, and the light grew brighter, and they swayed back and forth like the corn. Afterwards, they all fell silent again—but the silence was soon broken by an odd, repetitive sound coming from above. As if in a trance, no one thought to try and identify its source, until it was practically on top of them. A helicopter was hovering over the circle. Heidegger looked up and saw the fat, remorseless face of J. Edgar Hoover staring down at him. Hoover stuck a bullhorn out the window: "Nobody move!"

All at once everyone except Heidegger and Mishima scattered in all directions, disappearing into the tall corn. Manson turned back momentarily. "It was nice knowing you, Doc. But there's no way I'm goin' back to the big house."

"Where are you headed?" called Heidegger, genuinely sorry to see him go.

"The Hamptons," Manson said, holding up a fork. "Those people out there need me." And then he vanished into the corn.

The helicopter touched down in the circle and Heidegger and Mishima boarded it. After they had buckled in, Hoover handed

"Chicago"

Heidegger an envelope.

"What's this?" asked Heidegger.

"Your plane ticket to Germany. You leave this evening. I'm sorry, Professor Heidegger, but you're just too hot to handle."

Heidegger took the envelope, smiling slightly at the unintended compliment.

Then Hoover addressed himself to Mishima. "As for you, sir, I'm taking you into my personal custody. Clyde and I would love to dine with you . . ."

The helicopter lifted off, and for the first time Heidegger felt he could relax. His American journey was almost over, and he would be returning to his beloved Black Forest. In a few short minutes, the copter would be at O'Hare, leaving the sunlit miracle of the cornfield behind, and leaving Heidegger in Chicago.

ABOUT THE AUTHOR

Jef Costello is a writer based in New York City. His many essays and reviews have appeared at *North American New Right*, the webzine of Counter-Currents Publishing (www.counter-currents.com). He is also the author of *The Importance of James Bond & Other Essays* (San Francisco: Counter-Currents, 2015). His writings have been translated into German, French, Russian, and Swedish.

www.ingramcontent.com/pod-product-compliance
Lightning Source LLC
Chambersburg PA
CBHW030343131224
18858CB00004B/149